Who's Who in Faeryland

JOHN KRUSE

GREEN MAGIC

Green Magic

53 Brooks Road

Street

Somerset

BA16 0PP

England

www.greenmagicpublishing.com

ISBN 978-1-7399733-4-6

Designed & typeset by Carrigboy, Wells, UK

www.carrigboy.co.uk

GREEN MAGIC

Contents

CONTENTS

CHAPTER ONE

Foreword – A Wealth of Faeries

This book offers a series of biographies of some of the most significant and best-known of the faery folk. A lot of faeries are extremely familiar to us, being distinct characters with names and personalities. This *Who's Who* examines their origins, characters and development, from traditional folklore through to modern literature and the fine arts. In addition, it describes some of the less well-known faery individuals as well as faery beings that are named, but are really types or species.

What's revealed, amongst other things, is how deeply entrenched in our culture (and in our perceptions of Faery) many of these individuals have become. Many people know of the important role that William Shakespeare played in popularising these figures. The later work of other famous authors such as Sir Walter Scott may be less well recognised, but he deployed Titania, Oberon and Puck in many of his stories, helping to revive and consolidate their reputations for his and later generations.[1] Many other far less well-known poets have since embraced these names, demonstrating how completely they have been absorbed into our consciousness, often becoming symbols of Faery as a whole rather than individual personae.

THE DENHAM LIST

Michael Aislabie Denham (1801–1859) was an English merchant and collector of folklore. In the early part of his life, he conducted his business in Hull; later he set up as a general merchant at

---

1 See, for example, *The Bridal of Triermain, Rokeby*, canto LV & *Marmion*, canto LI.

Piercebridge, Co. Durham. In both places, he collected all sorts of local lore – sayings, songs and folktales – much of which he self-published. After his death many of his works were collected together and republished between 1846 and 1859 by the newly established Folklore Society as 'The Denham Tracts.'

Denham recorded many valuable scraps of material. One of the most fascinating of these, found in the second volume of the *Tracts*, is a list of fairies and evil spirits. He drew upon a short list already compiled by Reginald Scot in *The Discoverie of Witchcraft* (1584), perhaps supplementing this with another list found in George Gascoigne's play *The Buggbears* (1565), and then adding many additional terms from his own researches, to produce an encyclopaedic inventory, which reads as follows:

"Grose observes, too, that those born on Christmas Day cannot see spirits; which is another incontrovertible fact. What a happiness this must have been seventy or eighty years ago and upwards, to those chosen few who had the good luck to be born on the eve of this festival of all festivals; when the whole earth was so overrun with ghosts, boggles, bloody-bones, spirits, demons, ignis fatui, brownies, bugbears, black dogs, spectres, shellycoats, scarecrows, witches, wizards, barguests, Robin-Goodfellows, hags, night-bats, scrags, breaknecks, fantasms, hob-goblins, hobhoulards, boggy-boes, dobbies, hob-thrusts, fetches, kelpies, warlocks, mock-beggars, mum-pokers, Jemmy-burties, urchins, satyrs, pans, fauns, sirens, tritons, centaurs, calcars, nymphs, imps, incubusses, spoorns, men-in-the-oak, hell-wains, fire-drakes, kit-a-can-sticks, Tom-tumblers, melch-dicks, larrs, kitty-witches, hobby-lanthorns, Dick-a-Tuesdays, Elf-fires, Gyl-burnt-tails, knockers, elves, raw-heads, Meg-with-the-wads, old-shocks, ouphs, pad-foots, pixies, pictrees, giants, dwarfs, Tom-pokers, tutgots, snapdragons, sprats, spunks, conjurers, thurses, spurns, tantarrabobs, swaithes, tints, tod-lowries, Jack-in-the-Wads, mormos, changelings, redcaps, yett-hounds, colt-pixies, Tom-thumbs, black-bugs, boggarts, scar-bugs, shag-foals, hodge-pochers, hob-thrushes, bugs, bullbeggars, bygorns, bolls, caddies, bomen, brags, wraithes, waffs, flay-boggarts, fiends, gallytrots, imps, gytrashes, patches, hob-and-lanthorns, gringes, boguests, bonelesses, Peg-powlers, pucks, fays, kidnappers, gally-beggars, hudskins, nickers, madcaps, trolls, robinets, friars' lanthorns, silkies, cauld-lads, death-hearses, goblins, hob-headlesses, buggaboes, kows or cowes, nickies, nacks, waiths, miffies, buckles, gholes, sylphs, guests, swarths, freiths, freits, gy-carlins, pigmies, chittifaces, nixies, Jinny-burnt-tails, dudmen, hell-hounds, dopple-gangers, boggleboes, bogies, redmen, portunes, grants, hobbits, hobgoblins, brown-men, cowies, dunnies, wirrikows, alholdes, mannikins, follets, korreds, lubberkins, cluricanns, kobolds, leprechauns, kors, mares, korreds, puckles, korigans, sylvans, succubuses, black-men, shadows, banshees, lian-banshees, clabbernappers, Gabriel-hounds, mawkins, doubles, corpse lights or candles, scrats, mahounds, trows, gnomes, sprites, fates, fiends, sybils, nick-nevins, whitewomen, fairies, thrummy-caps, cutties and nisses, and apparitions of every shape, make, form, fashion, kind and description, that there was not a village in England that had not its own peculiar ghost. Nay, every lone tenement, castle, or mansion-house, which could boast of any antiquity had its bogle, its spectre, or its knocker. The churches, churchyards, and cross-roads, were all haunted. Every green lane had its boulder-stone on which an apparition kept watch at night. Every common had its circle of fairies belonging to it. And there was scarcely a shepherd to be met with who had not seen a spirit!"

This is a daunting catalogue, impressive (intimidating even) in its length and detail, and a little depressing in the sense that so many of the names now seem unfamiliar. It's clear how very rich the British fairy tradition once was, and how much has been lost in the last two hundred years.

Denham's list is, in a very real sense, an epitome of British faerylore. It includes a mixture of creatures from a range of sources: there are continental sprites, such as the Breton korigan and korred, classical beings that include satyrs, pans, fauns, sirens, tritons, nymphs and centaurs, Scandinavian trolls, Irish cluricanns and banshees, German kobolds and a variety of ghosts and ghouls. Just as English is a language that has borrowed extensively from French, Latin and other tongues, so British folklore is an amalgam.

The Denham cornucopia includes several faeries who must be mentioned in our *Who's Who*. Many that we might regard as essential entries in any such list are, nonetheless, absent. A large part of this explanation of this – as we shall see – is that many of them are, primarily or initially, literary characters. They enter our mythology from outside by the route of poems, plays, translations and novels. Some are foreign imports – such as Oberon and Titania; others are the invention of writers. Their contemporary fame prohibits that they be ignored as 'inauthentic'.

At the same time, I have decided to exclude from this account various fairies who will seem very familiar to readers. I don't mention leprechauns, for example, mainly because they are Irish rather than British fairies but also because they are renowned as a type or class but there are no truly famous leprechaun individuals, whose names and exploits are known to all. The same applies to mermaids: as a species they are very popular but there are no traditional characters with whom people are familiar – except for Hans Christian Anderson's *Little Mermaid*, a literary creature who bears little resemblance to the merfolk of folklore. For similar reasons gnomes and dwarves are excluded: they are not a true part of British folk tradition and there are no named individuals to discuss.

I have examined many of the themes discussed here in other books, but without the emphasis upon the individual characters themselves, which they receive here. Nonetheless, I recommend reference, too, to my studies on *Victorian Fairy Verse, Fairy Ballads and Rhymes, Fayerie* and *Fairy Art of the Twentieth Century Fairy* for further information on some of the topics covered and – especially – for the texts of many of the poems mentioned. Other references are given in the text.

CHAPTER TWO

What's in a Name?

If we are going to discuss the best-known individuals in British faeryland, by definition we need to be able to name them – and we shall: Mab, Oberon, Robin Goodfellow and others. That said, faeries are frequently very reluctant to let humans know their names and, as we shall see, many of the faeries encountered in British folklore are nameless or – for the practical convenience of mortals – bear names that we have given to them.

FAIRY NAMING PRACTICES

An initial matter to consider is faery language. Whilst sources make it clear that the faeries tend to be perfectly fluent in local human tongues and dialects, whether this may be English, Welsh, Manx, Gaelic or the speech of Orkney and Shetland, it is also frequently reported that they have their own, unknown languages as well. From this it must follow that some faeries may be named in their own tongue but that others may bear names that have been borrowed from the human population – or, at least – are used when dealing with humans because their own names might seem too difficult for us to pronounce.[1]

In the ballad of *Tam Lin*, a handsome human boy has been abducted to Elfland to serve in the fairy queen's retinue. His sweetheart, Janet, agrees to help save him and bring him home but he warns her of the obstacles she will face in attempting this. The fairies will change his form to try to scare her, but additionally he advises her:

---

1 For more on this, see my *British Fairies*, 2017, c.3; *Faery*, 2020, c.4 & *Manx Faeries*, 2021, c.1.

"First, they did call me Jack, he said,
And then they called me John,
But since I lived in the fairy court
Tomlin has always been my name."

These lines very strongly imply that, as part of his kidnapping and detention, a change of name has played a part – almost as a spell to keep him in Faery.

Names have considerable power in Faery. Knowing a name – or bestowing a name – is a source of power. This is demonstrated very well in a story from Clochfoldich Farm near Pitlochry. The farm's brownie would paddle and splash about in the burn near the farm until everyone had gone to bed; then he would come into the house with his wet feet to do his chores. The household nicknamed him Puddlefoot and one night the farmer came across him paddling in the stream and addressed him by the name. The brownie was so dismayed by the fact that he'd been named and might be subject to human control that he vanished for ever. Fairies often conceal their names in order from humans to preserve their power, but are as often careless in doing so, meaning that they are outwitted in the end. Welsh brownie *Gwarwyn-a-throt* exemplifies this: he is overheard by his intended victim foolishly repeating his name to himself, gloating that it is a secret – and so he is undone. In another example, from Wales, possession of the fairy maiden's name constrained her to marry the man who discovered it.[2]

Concealment of identity by this simple strategy is found in another ballad, *The Knight and the Shepherd's Daughter*, although in this case a seducer is trying to avoid taking any responsibility for a child he has fathered. Before he leaves her, the knight is asked for his name by the shepherdess and he responds, evasively:

"Some men do call me Jack, sweetheart,
And some do call me John;

---

2 Briggs, *Personnel of Fairyland*, 1953, 127; Rhys, *Celtic Folklore*, 45; see too my *British Fairies*, c.19.

But when I come to the King's fair court,
They call me Sweet William."

The lines in this ballad and in that of *Tam Lin* are obviously very similar; there may well have been borrowing from one song to another, in fact. Nonetheless, this shouldn't detract from the significance of personal names in Faery.

For that matter, similar magic applies to human names, which should in all cases be withheld from the faes. There is a class of stories, the so-called 'ainsel' theme, which hinges upon this point. A human meets a fairy of some description and, on being asked his/her name, cannily responds 'mi ainsel,' 'misen' or the Gaelic equivalent *'mi-fhín'* (all meaning 'myself'). In response, the faery is similarly wary and taciturn. Some dispute then arises between them, the human fends of the fairy's attack and injures it and the fairy flees to complain to a parent or to its companions. They are unsympathetic, because the aggrieved fae has to admit that it was 'myself' who inflicted the harm. This story involves simple self-preservation, but concealing a name is a more general protection against supernatural control. Put simply, if the fairies have a grievance against you, it's harder for them to find you if they don't have your name!

A name can, therefore, be a source of power and of protection. It follows that the fairies would very likely want to change an abductee's name when that person is safely 'under the hill,' so as to make it harder for family and friends to retrieve him or her. There could well be another aspect to this too, though. The harsh truth is that, for many visitors to Elfame, the experience is an unpleasant and involuntary one. They are taken as captives and held in servitude, performing chores for the fairies (whether child rearing or kitchen duties) that are never-ending and exhausting. Such conditions can only be called slavery and it has, of course, been the practice of human slave masters throughout history to rename their slaves, taking away their individuality and rendering them more clearly someone else's property. It would make sense for the faes to do the same: if they have a human skivvying in the kitchens, or serving at banquets, they have to be able to call them something, but they may very well wish to avoid using their proper personal names.

Finally, we ought to recognise that fairy expert Lewis Spence felt uncertain about the significance of the lines in *Tam Lin*. He had made a wide study of British and world folklore and could not think of other examples of a name change being part of the magical detention of a captive. Nevertheless, he also observed that in some versions of the ballad Janet has to keep calling out Tam's name as she undertakes his rescue, further suggesting that there is some spell residing in the unearthly name that has to be broken to free the boy from the fairy queen's clutches.

FAERY NAMES

It follows from what's just been said that most traditional fairies are anonymous – they guard their names from humans as a source of power. The spinning stories in which a fairy's name has to be guessed (Rumpelstiltskin, Perrifool etc., for whom see later) are examples which demonstrate magical conservation of a name combined with a fascinating sample of fairy names.

In the catalogue of recorded fairy names, what's fictional and fanciful is entangled and entwined with what's derived from tradition and personal encounters. It's very hard to separate out the jokey, made-up names, the ones that are modelled on classical Greek or Roman or Biblical sources, the everyday human names and those few that don't sound like anything familiar at all – and so, perhaps, are the most authentic.

The classical type of name was especially popular in Renaissance times. A late sixteenth century charm used to summon the faeries for sex and in order to help find buried treasure called on the "seven sisters of the fairies" who were named Lilia, Hestilia, Fata, Sola, Afrya, Julia and Venulla.[3]

In the *Discoverie of Witchcraft* of 1584, Reginald Scot mentioned only three faery sisters who might assist magicians in their conjuring, but they have names that are similarly vaguely Latin or classical: Milia, Archilia and Sibylia. His near

---

3 Sloane 3850, ff.145–166.

contemporary William Lilly one time tried to conjure the queen of fairies, whom he called Micol and which sounds very like Hebrew.

About seventy years after Scot, witch suspect Isobel Gowdie told her trial that she had met a number of elves, whose names were Robert the Jakis, Sanderis the Read Reaver, Thomas the Fearie and Robert the Rule. The ballad *Hind Etin* supplies another name of the period, Etin being the fae's given name coupled with 'hind,' an Old English word denoting a country boy or farm servant. The brownie of Bladnoch in Wigtownshire was called Aiken Drum, whilst a brownie known in the Ochil Hills of Central Scotland was Tod Lowrie or Red Bonnet. The latter title was clearly a human designation; the former might be more authentically faery.[4]

From Stornoway on Shetland, we hear a number of Gaelic names, many of which seem to be nicknames or were perhaps names used to avoid saying the fay's true name: there are *Deocan nam Beann* (milkwort), *Popar, Peulagan* and *Conachay* (little conch). The trows of the northern isles have a variety of names, some of which retain hints of Viking Norse whilst others just sound like nicknames: Gimp, Kork, Tring, Tivla, Fivla, Hornjultie, Peester-a-leeti, Skoodern Humpi, Bannock Feet and Hempie the Ferry-louper. On the Isle of Man, we hear of a fairy king called (prosaically) Philip and his queen, Bahee, which is at least exotic enough to sound more authentic.

Spiritualist Daphne Charters claimed to have met a vast number of nature spirits, amongst whom were numbered Normus, Gorgus, Myrris, Movus, Mirilla, Namsos, Sirilla, Nuvic, Nixus, Lyssis, Tanchon and Persion. She also encountered two Chinese fairies who rejoiced in the fairly un-Oriental names of Perima and Sulac. Charters' great friend and supporter, Air Chief Marshall Dowding, was puzzled by the Latin sounding names of many of these fays, but he concluded that the simple explanation was that the Romans had adopted fairy names, not the other way around![5]

---

4 Pitcairn, *Ancient Criminal Trials in Scotland*, vol.3, Part 2, 602; R Menzies Fergusson, *Ochil Folk Tales*, 1912, 'The story of the brownie.'
5 Charters, *A True Fairy Tale*, 1956, c.2 & Foreword by Dowding.

Amongst the evidence of witnesses recorded by Marjorie Johnson and published as *Seeing Fairies,* we encounter a "little creature named Peto [who] lived on the canopy over Miss Hannah Jackson's dining room fireplace in Manchester." In addition, she reports an elf called Etto who lived in a ruined castle in Leicestershire but regularly visited the witness in her home, a Shropshire fae called Hartha, and two faeries in Queensland called Penelo and, rather more prosaically, Valerie.[6]

Our newest evidence comes from the recently completed *Fairy Census.* The names recorded by witnesses are, like those in Johnson's book, a mix of the conventional and bizarre. Fairies variously identified themselves to witnesses as Effeny, Sylvizz, La Belle Courtland, Goldenrod, Zee and Specia.[7]

We have a spectrum here from the everyday, through the traditional, to the mildly exotic. What emerges seems to be a mixture of classical inherited names, conventional contemporary names and some which might be dismissed as made up or might alternatively be thought of as examples of genuine fairy appellations. It's a puzzling mixture, contrasting with the fairly high degree of consensus over fairy dress and appearance.

Perhaps what we can identify in this catalogue are the close parallels with the nature of the language spoken: sometimes it's familiar, sometimes archaic, occasionally it is unknown and hard to understand. There may well be problems for us humans reproducing the sounds and combinations we hear in fairy names, causing us to substitute something more familiar and pronounceable.

> "Be careful how ye speake here o' the Wee Folk,
> Or they will play such pranks on thee and thine,
> Nae doubt, they dae a lot of good whiles,
> But if provoked, they can be maist unkind."[8]

If you do come to know the name of a fairy, it should always be treated with the utmost respect and care, like a closely guarded

---

6 Johnson, *Seeing Fairies*, 2014, 72, 157, 219 & 256.
7 *Census* numbers 117, 244, 307, 326, 383 and 438.
8 Henry Terrell, *The Wee Folk of Menteith*, 46.

secret. Fairy names are a taboo subject: they are a source of power and must be handled circumspectly.

HUMAN NAMES FOR FAERIES

I have attempted in the last section to assemble a list of what may be authentic faery personal names, but I recognise that many of those cited as still likely to have been given by humans.

Turning to names that were definitely bestowed upon faeries by their mortal neighbours, as a way of referring to the supernatural living near them, we might begin by mentioning the murderous boggart Jeanie of Biggersdale who resided in Mulgrave Wood near Whitby in North Yorkshire and who would pursue and attack travellers. Rather more locally, the boggart that haunted the village of Bolhot, near Bury, and specifically Whittle Lane, was called the Whittle Bol. It seems that the second element isn't derived from the placename; by merest coincidence, boll, bolly, or bolleroy are all other terms for bogle. Another local being was, even more generically, the Hob i' th' Wood.[9]

The brownie of Tullochgorm Castle in Strathspey seems to bear a human appellation: she's variously referred to as Maug Moulach, Meg Mullach or Maggie Moloch. Margaret is plainly a human first name, whilst the second element is an adjective from the Gaelic, *moloch,* meaning 'hairy' when describing an animal. I've already mentioned Puddlefoot the a Perthshire brownie, very evidently named descriptively because he lived in a small burn between Pitlochry and Dunkeld. He performed chores for a nearby farm, leaving wet footprints – hence the name. When he learned what the humans called him, he vanished and was never seen again. It seems clear from the accounts that these names were not chosen by the faery beings but were designated by the humans who had contact with them – as Puddlefoot's aggrieved reaction confirms.

9 George Young, *History of Whitby*, 1817, vol.2, 883; *Manchester Times*, Nov. 2nd 1850, 3; on boggarts generally see my *Beyond Faery*, 2020.

Joan Willimot of Goadby in Leicestershire was tried for witchcraft in 1616. Amongst her evidence were the details of her familiar spirit, a fairy woman called Pretty who had been blown into her mouth by her former master. Pretty seems more likely to be an affectionate name bestowed by Willimot than the spirit's actual, given name – though you never know. Perhaps the name of this familiar spirit is a further example of the general prettification of fays that has set in since the Mustardseed and Peaseblossom of Shakespeare's *Midsummer Night's Dream*. The same process also seems to have given us the Moonbeam and Dewdrop mentioned in Bowker's *Goblin Tales*; similar whimsy and a sense of harmony may have produced the Modilla and Podilla mentioned on Dartmoor by Crossing.[10]

Over the years, a number of fairy infants have been found lost and have been taken in by humans for short periods of time. Amongst them have been Bobby Griglans and Coleman Grey in Cornwall, Shilo in Devon, Brother Mike in East Anglia and Hewie Milburn and Gilpin Horner in Scotland. Most of these names seem to be bestowed by the finders: Bobby for example, was found asleep on a bank of 'griglans' (heath), although this word is a variant of 'grig' which is listed by Denham as being one of the more obscure British supernaturals. Be that as it may, when Bobby's parents came looking for him, they called out for 'Skillywidden.' This, and Shilo, might perhaps be authentic names. A related story tells of the child faery called Malekin, who for a while haunted Dagworthy Castle in Suffolk. 'Mal' is an old pet form of Mary, so that I suspect that the name was again given by the humans, meaning 'little Mary.'[11]

Playful names that shouldn't be taken seriously at all are very common. In 1627 in *Nimphidia* Drayton listed Hop, Mop, Dryp, Pip, Trip, Skip, Fib, Tib, Pinch, Pin, Tick, Quick, Jil, Jin, Tit, Nit, Wap and Win. The following year, the *Life of Robin Goodfellow* added Patch, Gull, Grim, Sib, Licke and Lull. These are very evidently writer's names, invented for the sound and

---

10 William Crossing, *Tales of Dartmoor Pixies*, 1890.
11 *Denham Tracts*, vol.2; see my *Faery* (2020) and *Faery Lifecycle* (2021).

for the occasional lewd connotation – as with the faery Pricke in John Lyly's *Maids Metamorphosis* (1600): he is a little faery who frightens all the wenches out of their beds ...

Professor John Rhys recorded a tradition from Eryri (Snowdonia) to the effect that a local family was "known by the nickname of *Pellings* ... a word corrupted from their [faery] mother's name, Penelope."[12] This name is problematic, as it's Greek – being the name of Ulysses' wife – and it was not used in Britain until the late sixteenth century.[13] It might perhaps be an equivalent to a Welsh name, just as in Ireland Penelope was used as an alternative to *Fionnguala* (Finola); it might, instead, be a local invention. In this respect, compare the story of the folk healer (and fantasist) Mary Parrish, who in the 1680s managed to convince the wealthy gentleman Goodwin Wharton that she was in contact with the faeries that dwelt beneath Hounslow Heath near London. Leading figures in the faery court were King Byron, Queen Penelope LaGard and Princess Ursula LaPerle. These French names sound pretty suspicious, although Parrish perhaps did better with two evil spirits she said she had discovered, Rumbonium and Bromka.[14]

NURSERY SPRITES

A special category of named faeries is the class of so-called 'nursery sprites.' Many of the dangerous water sprites who haunt pools and rivers around Britain are named: Jenny Greenteeth, Peg O'Nell, Peg Powler, Nelly Long Arms, Jenny Hurn, Jenny on't Boggart, Mary Hosies and Nicky Nicky Nye. In truth, the last of these may not be a true name but may derive instead from 'nicker' or 'nixie,' a sort of river sprite.

Labels for wills of the wisp similarly include human first names, such as Jenny Burnt Arse, Dicke a Tuesday, Jemmy Burtie, Jacky Lantern, Peg a Lantern, Meg with the Wad and

---

12 Rhys, vol.1, 48, citing Williams 37–40; see too my *Faery Lifecycle*, 2021.
13 Johnson & Sleigh, *Names for Boys & Girls*, 1962, *sub nom.*
14 For the full story of Parrish, see my *How Things Work in Faery*, 2021.

Jack in the Wad, Dank Will, Kitty with a Wisp, Kit with the Canstick and Gyl Burnt-Tayle.[15]

Amongst the faeries that guard orchards from depredations is Lazy Lawrence. It might be worthwhile noting that the pixies of the New Forest were generically named Lawrence and that of a lazy person it might be said that 'Lawrence is on him.' As we'll note later, a horse-like manifestation of puck that protected apple harvests in this area was the colt-pexy.[16] Other sprites protecting orchards include Churnmilk Peg and Melsh Dick.

One nursery sprite, associated with getting children to go to sleep, was Wee Willie Winky. He was publicised by Scot William Miller, who in 1841 first published the famous rhyme concerning Willie, in which he runs up and down stairs throughout the town to check that the 'wee uns' are in bed by ten o'clock. Billy Winker was the Lancashire equivalent of this sprite. Willie is a kind and gentle spirit, whereas Tom Dockin and Tom Poker were fearsome beings who lurked in dark places waiting to scare and even devour naughty and disobedient infants.

Another household sprite, Billy Blind, offered wise counsel rather than performing specific tasks or being used to scare children into compliance. In the ballad of *Young Bekie,* he also appears to possess some prophetic powers or magical knowledge – a reasonably common faery trait, but one that is strangely at odds with his second name.

What's most noticeable about the foregoing lists is the prevalence of certain first names: Jenny, Jack, Kit, Will, Gill, Peg, and Dick. These are all diminutives of names that were extremely common in Britain from medieval times until quite recently: John, Joan, Katherine, William, Gillian, Richard and Margaret. What this suggests is that common and colloquial names were applied to sprites in an effort to diminish the distance between mortals and supernaturals, to try to make them seem less intimidating and, through a sense of friendly familiarity, to try to befriend or pacify them.

---

15 *Gentleman's Magazine*, 1881, vol.250, 335.
16 *Southampton Herald*, May 27th 1893, 2 'New Forest, Local Superstitions.'

It should be added, too, that the most significant aspect of this naming process was that it applied to faeries as a class, rather than to individuals. These nursery sprites – and the wills of the wisp and river spirits earlier mentioned – are not single manifestations but are widespread across the whole of Britain. This sets them very clearly apart from the named characters whom we will examine for the remainder of this book.

CHAPTER THREE

Queen Mab

First and foremost, the queen of British Faery is Mab. She may very well be a homegrown monarch, perhaps descending ultimately from the Irish/ British goddess Medb/Maeve. Her ancestry isn't wholly clear and it has been proposed too that she might be related to the continental queen of the fairies and witches, Lady Habundia or Dame Abonde.[1]

Whatever her origins, by the sixteenth century, when fairies appear in English literature, there is little question that Mab is queen.[2] Her centrality and ubiquity may be indicated by the fact that 'Mab-led' exists as an alternative to the better-known phrase 'pixie-led.' Just like Puck, or the Will of the Wisp, Mab could be blamed for leading travellers astray, thereby acting as an elemental fairy force. Ben Jonson knew of this tradition when he included it amongst her pastimes: "And then leads them, from her borroughs,/ Home through ponds, and water furrowes."[3]

LUSTY MAB

In her passion for Bottom and her alleged affection for Theseus, the newly-crowned queen Titania inherited much of the wanton sexuality of fairies generally and especially that of Queen Mab. She was, however, a rather pale imitation of her rather more earthy predecessor. For example, in Drayton's 1627 epic

---

1 Robert Burton, in his *Anatomy of Melancholy*, Part I, section 2, names Habundia as the queen of the 'water devils' – the naiads, water nymphs or fairies.

2 Note, however, that in Sloane MS 1727, a seventeenth century magical text held by the British Library, Mab is demoted to the position of "Lady to the Queen," the monarch herself remaining unnamed.

3 Jonson, *Entertainment at Althorpe*, also called *The Satyr*, 1603.

Nimphidia, Mab is connected to much older images of the nocturnal succubus:

> "And Mab, his merry queen, by night
> Bestrides young folks that lie upright,
> (In elder times the mare that hight)
> Which plagues them out of measure."

The fairy queen as bringer of sexual nightmares seems to have been a longstanding aspect of her character. Shelley was later to crown her the queen of dreams in his poem *Queen Mab* and Shakespeare in *Romeo and Juliet* (1597) openly celebrated this trait:

> "This is the hag, when maids lie on their backs,
> that presses them and learns them first to bear,
> making them women of good carriage."

It's pretty evident the playwright saw Mab as having a function as a sexual educator for virgins, showing them how to perform in bed and maybe even seducing them in the process. That bearing, or carriage, is not about deportment but about receiving a lover lying on top; for men, meanwhile, if they are found 'upright' at night, the queen would also straddle them and further their sexual initiation, as we've just seen.[4]

Mab was, therefore, a more traditional British figure and she was by no means eclipsed by the success of her upstart rival. Her amorous nature lies at the heart of the plot in Drayton's *Nimphidia*. The queen is "faire" and she arouses the love of courtier Pigwiggen. He sends her a bracelet as a gift and invites her to meet him secretly – something she eagerly agrees to – "she by nothing might be stayde,/ For naught must her be letting." At their tryst "The Queene, bound with Loves powerfulst charme,/ Sate with Pigwiggen arme in arme," In fact, it seems matters went rather further than that, because later she is awoken by Puck's voice, a detail strongly suggestive of a post-coital slumber.

---

4 Act I, 4.

The queen was widely praised for her good looks – but then, the irresistible charms of fairy women, and most especially their queens, were another longstanding convention of faery lore. In Thomas Randolph's *Amyntas* (dated to about 1632), Mab is described as "beauteous Empresse."[5] She also described as "joyall" but there is, as well, a hint of her reputation for infidelity.[6]

QUEEN OF DREAMS & DAIRIES

Mab seems to have had two traditional functions, then, as a maker of dreams and as a domestic goddess, helping or punishing maids according to their cleanliness. Shakespeare's mention of her in *Romeo and Juliet* elaborates upon the former role:

> "And, in this state, she gallops night by night
> Through lovers' brains, and then they dream of love;
> O'er courtiers' knees, that dream on court'sies straight,
> O'er lawyers' fingers, who straight dream on fees,
> O'er ladies ' lips, who straight on kisses dream,
> Which oft the angry Mab with blisters plagues,
> Because their breaths with sweetmeats tainted are:
> Sometime she gallops o'er a courtier's nose,
> And then dreams he of smelling out a suit;
> And sometime comes she with a tithe-pig's tail
> Tickling a parson's nose as a' lies asleep,
> Then dreams, he of another benefice:
> Sometime she driveth o'er a soldier's neck,
> And then dreams he of cutting foreign throats,
> Of breaches, ambuscadoes, Spanish blades,
> Of healths five-fathom deep; and then anon
> Drums in his ear, at which he starts and wakes,
> And being thus frighted swears a prayer or two
> And sleeps again."[7]

---

5 Act II, 6, also Act I, 3; see too Randolph's *Jealous Lovers* Act III, scene 7 in which Asotus praises her as "Mab, my Empresse fair."

6 Act I, 3 & II, 7.

7 *Romeo & Juliet*, Act I, 4.

Thomas Randolph also made reference to her connection with dreams in his play *Hey for Honesty, Down with Knavery*. Dicaeus, a priest, recalls a recent dream which seems to have been fulfilled:

> "Last night I laughed in my sleep. The queen of fairy tickled my nose with a tithe-pig's tale. I dreamt of another benefice and see how it comes about!"[8]

An anonymous poem, *The Holly Bush*, which was published in 1646, describes Mab the tyrannous fairy pinching wenches (see later), before turning to address her role in dreams:[9]

> "Some the night-mare hath prest
> With that weight on their breast,
> No returnes of their breath can passe;
> But to us the tale is addle,
> We can take off her saddle,
> And turne out the night-mare to grasse."

It may be added that this power over dreams was also something ascribed to Robin Goodfellow/ Puck (for whom see later). In *Robin Goodfellow, his Mad Pranks* of 1628 there is reference to his influence – both benign and malign. Robin can take the form of the bellman, or nightwatchman, who cries "May you dream of your delights/ In your sleeps, see pleasing sights;" but he is also linked to the nightmare: "Now doe young wenches sleepe/ Til their dreams wake them."

Meanwhile, in her more domestic persona, Queen Mab and her fairy court not only supervised the activities of dairy maids but avidly consumed the produce those maids had slaved over. Thomas Randolph, Ben Jonson and Milton, in *L' Allegro*, all alluded to Mab's taste for such dairy products as cream and junkets. So great was this that she resorted to theft to get them if she had to or would hinder dairy production if she chose.[10]

---

8 Randolph, *A Pleasant Comedie, entituled Hey for Honesty, Down with Knavery, translated out of Aristophanes his Plutus*, Act II, scene 6.

9 'The Holly Bush,' in *Men Miracles with Other Poems*, London, 1646.

10 For example, Randolph, *Amyntas*, IV, 4, Jonson, *The Satyr*, 1603; Milton, *L'Allegro*, 102.

All in all, Mab was often quite unregal in her behaviour. She got directly involved in human affairs, meddling personally with the humblest of household servants and in the most ordinary of domestic tasks. This is encapsulated in Robert Herrick's charming synopsis of the principal tenets of English fairy belief, *The Fairies:*

> "If ye will with Mab find grace,
> Set each platter in his place;
> Rake the fire up, and get
> Water in, ere sun be set.
>
> Wash your pails and cleanse your dairies;
> Sluts are loathsome to the fairies;
> Sweep your house, who doth not so,
> Mab will pinch her by the toe."

According to Ben Jonson, the queen also indulged in stealing human babies (leaving ladles in their stead) and in luring midwives out of their beds in their sleep.[11]

This less than queenly conduct may surprise modern readers, but it seemed to be much less remarkable at the time. Several of the women tried as suspected witches in Scotland during the same period gave confessions to their inquisitors that featured just such homely conduct from their queens of Elfame.

MINIATURE MAB

Although her sexual contacts with humans very much indicate that Mab would be encountered in the form of a fully grown woman, she was subject to the miniaturisation that began to afflict all fairy queens. We see this applied to Titania in *Midsummer Night's Dream,* whom Oberon describes as sleeping on a flowery bank where "the snake throws her enamell'd skin/ Wide enough to wrap a fairy in" and whose servants creep into

---

11 Jonson, *The Satyr.*

acorn cups to hide from the king's anger.[12] In fact, Shakespeare had already initiated this shrinkage for Mab during Mercutio's soliloquy about her in *Romeo and Juliet,* first performed in 1597:

> "O, then, I see Queen Mab hath been with you.
> She is the fairies' midwife, and she comes
> In shape no bigger than an agate-stone
> On the fore-finger of an alderman,
> Drawn with a team of little atomies
> Athwart men's noses as they lie asleep;
> Her wagon-spokes made of long spiders' legs,
> The cover of the wings of grasshoppers,
> The traces of the smallest spider's web,
> The collars of the moonshine's watery beams,
> Her whip of cricket's bone, the lash of film,
> Her wagoner a small grey-coated gnat,
> Not so big as a round little worm
> Prick'd from the lazy finger of a maid;
> Her chariot is an empty hazel-nut
> Made by the joiner squirrel or old grub,
> Time out o' mind the fairies' coachmakers...
> ... This is that very Mab
> That plats the manes of horses in the night,
> And bakes the elflocks in foul sluttish hairs,
> Which once untangled, much misfortune bodes:"

Mab here is a tiny being and also one, like many other pixies and fairies, who likes to take horses from stables at night to ride them, knotting their manes into bridles and stirrups.

Michael Drayton and Robert Herrick consolidated this miniaturising trend. In *Nimphidia* the queen travels to her lover's assignation with Pigwiggen in a cowslip flower by riding in a miniscule carriage:

---

12 *Dream*, Act II, 1.

"Foure nimble Gnats the Horses were,
Their Harnasses of Gossamere,
Flye Cranion her Chariottere,
Upon the Coach-box getting.

Her Chariot of a Snayles fine shell,
Which for the colours did excell:
The faire Queene Mab, becomming well,
So lively was the limming:
The seate the soft wooll of the Bee;
The cover (gallantly to see)
The wing of a pyde Butterflee,
I trowe t'was simple trimming.

The wheeles compos'd of Crickets bones,
And daintily made for the nonce,
For feare of ratling on the stones,
With Thistle-downe they shod it ..."

Herrick continued this theme. In *Oberon's Palace* Mab lies on her bed as she awaits her drunken husband's arrival. She looks "as tender as a chick" as she reclines:

"Upon six plump Dandillions ...
Whose woollie-bubbles seem'd to drowne
Her Mab-ship in obedient Downe."

Her bed sheets were the cauls of babies and her blankets were of finest gossamer. Another of Herrick's poems is a plea for alms addressed by *The Beggar to Mab, the Fairie Queen.* He is poor and asks for scraps from her table – an ant, a bee's abdomen or a cricket's hip, for example.

MAB'S DOMINION

Even after the advent of Queen Titania, Mab's memory continued to be celebrated. Mab, the "mistris-Faerie," took a lead role before King James in Ben Jonson's masque *The Satyr,* performed in June 1603; she was the fairy queen in Drayton's *Muse's Elizium;* she leads the fairy dancing in the little poem *The Faery Queen* that was first published in *The Mysteries of Love and Eloquence,* 1658, and for Margaret Cavendish, Duchess of Newcastle, she was the monarch of her fairy verses, such as *Queen Mab's Dinner Table* or *The Pastime of the Queen of Fairies* – "There Mab is Queen of all, by Nature's will." This ruler is, all the same, miniature, being seated beneath a flower surrounded by the "Fairy fry" of her court.[13]

Interestingly, in his 1679 play *The History and Fall of Caius Marius,* Thomas Otway brazenly stole Mercutio's speech from *Romeo and Juliet,* putting it in the mouth of Roman Sulpitius with only modest alterations and very much retaining Mab's tininess. Much more recently, American poet and dramatist Richard Hovey (1864–1900) commandeered from Shakespeare not just Mab but Puck, Oberon, Titania *and* Ariel for his rather curious verse-play *The Quest of Merlin – A Prelude.*[14]

Mab's position and popularity were not diminished for later generations – despite the enhanced profile granted to Titania.[15] Charlotte Dacre (1771–1825), perpetuated the miniscule Mab in her poem *Queen Mab and her Fays,* in which they transform themselves into flies and intervene in the dreams of human lovers. Musing upon a *Twilight Moth,* Madison Julius Cawein exclaimed:

> "Gnome – wrought of moonbeam – fluff and gossamer,
> Silent as scent, perhaps thou chariotest
> Mab or King Oberon; or, haply, her
> His queen, Titania, on some midnight quest."

The queen is tiny, too, in Thomas Hood's *The Plea of the Midsummer Fairies,* and it follows logically that this is also her consort's stature: "King Oberon, and all his merry crew / The

---

13 Jonson, *The Satyr,* 1603.

14 Published in 1891 as part of *Lancelot and Guenevere – A Poem in Dramas.*

15 *Fairyland,* George Barlow; *Puck to Queen Mab,* H. Sinclair Lewis; *Queen Mab in the Village,* Vachell Lindsay; *The Fairies' Passage,* James Mangan; *On Midsummer Night,* Madison Cawein; *Fairy Sky,* John Russell Hayes; *An Evening Dream,* Sydney Dobell.

darling puppets of Romance's view." Hood also described her as "stealthy Mab, queen of old realms romantic" and elsewhere as "glib," when describing her flights around the world. Curiously, she is present in Hood's poem alongside Queen Titania – though apparently without rancour. In Sydney Dobell's *Snowdrops*, she 'wings' through the night on a moth and the daisy of the poem of that name by Eric Mackay (1851–98) serves as "A mimic sun to light a true-love bower/ For fair Queen Mab."

In *Halloween, 1916* by Arthur Peterson, another of the monarch's traditional roles is recalled: "Mab who teases house-wives/ If their housewifery be wrong." She is still an entrancing beauty, too, as in Paul Dunbar's *The Discovery:* "Queen Mab was there, her shimmering hair/ Each fairy prince's heart's despair."

Against these verses faithful to the older sources, we must set Thomas Hood's *Queen Mab,* written in about 1842. The fairy queen he presents is far closer to the twee and girly fairies, found so much in contemporary culture, than to the robust and independent Mab of former times.

"A little fairy comes at night,
Her eyes are blue, her hair is brown,
With silver spots upon her wings,
And from the moon she flutters down.
She has a little silver wand,
And when a good child goes to bed
She waves her wand from right to left,
And makes a circle round its head.

And then it dreams of pleasant things,
Of fountains filled with fairy fish,
And trees that bear delicious fruit,
And bow their branches at a wish;

Of arbours filled with dainty scents
From lovely flowers that never fade;
Bright flies that glitter in the sun,
And glow-worms shining in the shade.

And talking birds with gifted tongues,
For singing songs and telling tales,
And pretty dwarfs to show the way
Through fairy hills and fairy dales.

But when a bad child goes to bed,
From left to right she weaves her rings,
And then it dreams all through the night
Of only horrid things!

Then lions come with glaring eyes,
And tigers growl, a dreadful noise,
And ogres draw their cruel knives
To shed the blood of girls and boys.

Then stormy waves rush on to drown,
Or raging flames come scorching round,
Fierce dragons hover in the air,
And serpents crawl along the ground.

Then wicked children wake and weep,
And wish the long black gloom away;
But good ones love the dark, and find
The night as pleasant as the day."

Hood retained Mab's link to dreams, but they have been divorced from the adult concerns with sex, cupidity and gain; rather, this delicate butterfly fairy acts as some adjunct to parental admonishments, enforcing a code of 'good' and 'bad' behaviour in the Victorian nursery.

As with so many of the other famous fairies, of course, Mab has increasingly been reduced to a fairy tale figure fit only for childish fancies, losing much of her mature significance and force.[16] Consequent upon that diminishment and trivialisation, there has been a growing tendency towards disbelief and dismissal. American author Emma Lazarus (1849–87) expressed this in her verse *August Moon*:

---

16 Sir Arthur Quiller Couch, *Of Three Children Choosing*.

"Ancient legends come to mind.
Who would marvel should he find,
In the copse or nigh the spring,
Summer fairies gambolling
Where the honey-bees do suck,
Mab and Ariel and Puck?
Ah! no modern mortal sees
Creatures delicate as these.
All the simple faith has gone
Which their world was builded on."

Despite Titania's ascendancy, Mab has also continued to appear in the visual arts. Turner exhibited *Queen Mab's Cave* in 1846, attaching to it a quotation from his own poem, *The Fallacies of Hope:* "Thy orgies, Mab, are manifold." Whatever he may have written, Turner's actual canvas is a lot less explicit. The picture is a golden sunset glow with very indistinct details; small naked figures are seen dancing and playing at the margins, but all we see in the cave itself is a bright shimmer of light and some hints of miniscule nudes.

The vision of the queen as a highly sexual being certainly comes through in the paintings of Swiss-born Henry Fuseli (Johann Heinrich Füssli, 1741–1825). His *Fairy Mab*, which was begun in 1793, is a surreal scene dominated by an adult sized queen dressed in gauzy fabrics which reveal her breasts and legs. She wears a crescent moon diadem, alluding to her connections to moon goddess Diana, and she seems to sit before a kind of lunar halo. Mab holds a bowl – presumably of milk or cream – from which she is eating with a spoon, but she pauses with her hand raised to her mouth, regarding us in a welcoming and rather seductive manner. The queen is surrounded by jugs and bowls from the dairy, as well as several other much smaller fairies. One of these has her face buried in a large bowl, another stands patiently by with her own bowl and spoon, awaiting her share of junket or such like.

Fuseli's *Queen Mab* of 1814 depicts a woman asleep on her couch. Mab is a diminutive figure in the background here, not immediately apparent; she has descended on a shaft of light, accompanied by moths and other fairy beings, and she waves her wand over the sleeper. The queen is conjuring the sleeper's dreams, and those are clearly sexual. The slumberer's shift has slipped down to reveal her breasts; to one side, on a dressing table, a tiny, naked female admires herself in the human woman's mirror, attended by another winged fae. Even more overtly sexual is the artist's *Mab Approaching Two Girls* (roughly dated 1800–20): the young women are naked in bed together, one being asleep whilst her partner admires and caresses her lover's body. Mab descends through parted curtains behind them, once again riding a beam of light. In the corner, a shadowy homunculus sits – perhaps a goblin. Such monstrosities are common in Fuseli's work, as (indeed) are erotic scenes. This particular picture forms a link between his illustrations of literature and his purely pornographic productions.

George Cruikshank, meanwhile, picked up upon the queen's role as a midwife of dreams. His *Queen Mab*, painted between 1850 and 1860, shows a tiny elfin band with flaming torches parading across a sleeper's face, an image very likely to have been derived from Shakespeare. Alfred Edward Chalon (1780–1860) was another Swiss artist who became established in Britain. His *Queen Mab* of 1827 also envisages the queen as maker of dreams: she is reduced to a miniature figure, floating above a sleeping woman in a miniscule boat and brandishing a very large wand over her victim. As an alternative vision, in 1906 Thomas Maybank painted a very rare picture inspired by Drayton's *Nimphidia*. In this gouache Mab is seen climbing into her carriage, ready for her assignation with Pigwiggen. She is a very dainty, blonde queen, with huge filmy butterfly wings, and scarcely looks like the lusty adulteress the poem suggests.

Lastly, Arthur Rackham illustrated Mab for a 1906 edition of *Romeo and Juliet*. His two portraits of the queen show a very different woman to most of the previous depictions – she is tall, elegant and serene. She wears white, flowing robes, her long hair tied up with jewelled ropes. She is far more regal than most of the visions of the monarch we have seen.

In conclusion, one final – and rather aberrant – literary appearance of the fairy queen must be mentioned. That is her role in the 1885 book, *That Very Mab,* by May Kendall and leading folklorist Andrew Lang. This is a very curious publication, a fairy story that has almost nothing to do with fairies; rather, it is a satire of British society in the penultimate decade of the nineteenth century.

In some senses the book is a sequel or parallel to *Titania's Farewell,* which I described earlier. In that story, the fairy court left England for good. The first chapter of *That Very Mab* discovers the queen living in Samoa:

> "England she had left long ago; when the Puritans arose, the fairies vanished. When 'Tom came home from labour and Cis from milking rose,' there was now no more sound of tabor, nor 'merrily went their toes.' Tom went to the Public House or the Preaching House, and Cis—Cis waited till Tom should come home and kick her into a jelly (his toes going merrily enough at that work), or tell her she was, spiritually, in a parlous case. So, the Fairy Queen and all her court had long since fled from England, and long ago made a home in the undiscovered isles of the South. Now they all met and mingled in the throng of the Polynesian fairy folk, and, rushing down into the waters, they revelled all night on the silvery sand, in the windless dancing places of the deep."

However, the modern world catches up with the queen in her island paradise: almost simultaneously British and German colonists arrive to claim and 'civilise' Polynesia. Mab decides to come back to Britain to see if her court has any hope of returning:

> "Queen Mab found England a good deal altered. There were still fairy circles in the grass; but they were attributed, not to fairy dances, but to unscientific farming and the absence of artificial phosphates. The country did not smell

of April and May, but of brick-kilns and the manufacture of chemicals. The rivers, which she had left bright and clear, were all black and poisonous. Water for drinking purposes was therefore supplied by convoys from the Apollinaris and other foreign wells, and it was thought that, if a war broke out, the natives of England would die of thirst. This was not the only disenchantment of Queen Mab. She found that in Europe she was an anachronism. She did not know, at first, what the word meant, but the sense of it gradually dawned upon her. Now there is always something uncomfortable about being an anachronism; but still people may become accustomed to it, and even take a kind of a pride in it, if they are only anachronisms on the right side – so far in the van of the bulk of humanity, for instance, that the bulk of humanity considers them not wholly in their right minds. There must surely be a sense of superiority in knowing oneself a century or two in front of one's fellow-creatures that counterbalances the sense of solitude. Queen Mab had no such consolation. She was an anachronism hundreds of years on the wrong side; in fact, a relic of Paganism."[17]

Mab reaches Epping Forest and meets a friendly owl who offers to guide her around the England of the 1880s. They start with a few barbed words about the attitude towards the natural world shown by the day-trippers who visit the Forest:

"They always leave the corks about, and confectionery paper bags, for the next people to gaze upon who come to worship Nature: you may see them now, if you look down. I have often thought those corks, and cigar-ends, and such tokens that the British public always leaves behind it, must be symbolical of something – offerings to Nature, you know, an invariable part of the rite…

'However,' he resumed, 'it is certain that their devotion is strong, and they offer to Nature the sacrifices dearest to

17 Chapter 2.

their own hearts, and probably dearest, therefore, to the heart of Nature. They cut their names all over her shrine, which is, I have no doubt, a welcome attention; but they do not look at her any more than they can help, for they stay where the beer is, and they are very warm, and flirt...'

'And does nobody believe in fairies?' sighed Queen Mab.

'No, or at least hardly anyone. A few of the children, perhaps, and a very, very few grown-up people – persons who believe in Faith-healing and Esoteric Buddhism, and Thought-reading, and Arbitration, and Phonetic Spelling, can believe in anything, except what their mothers taught them on their knees. All of these are in just now.'"

A series of vignettes follow, in which Queen Mab meets various representative characters from late Victorian society: a scientist, a bishop, a democrat, an anarchist and others. The book is full of topical references and in-jokes which will mean very little to most modern readers, although they may have been very amusing and piquant at the time.

Various digs are made at contemporary scientific rationalism as well as at the effects of education. For example:'

"The professor replied that fairies were unscientific, and even unthinkable, and the divine declared that they were too heterodox even for the advanced state of modern theology, and had been condemned by several councils, which is true. And the professor ran through all the animal kingdoms and sub-kingdoms very fast, and proved quite conclusively, in a perfect cataract of polysyllables, that fairies didn't belong to any of them."[18]

"He might have had more sense, then?' returned Queen Mab, still ruffled. 'He might have seen that I was a fairy. The child suspected something at once.'

'Ah, he was an exceptional child,' said the Owl. 'Most of the children, nowadays, don't believe anything. In fact,

---

18 Chapter 3.

now that education is spreading so widely, I don't suppose one of them will in ten years' time...'

'Tell me about the children,' said Queen Mab. 'I shall understand that better.'

'They have to learn facts, facts, forever facts,' said the Owl compassionately. 'It makes one's head ache to think of it...'"[19]

Later, that same 'exceptional child,' having attended a preparatory school for Eton, has lost all his romantic inclinations: "He said that bogies were all bosh" and he tries to bring down the fairy queen by throwing stones – and any other handy items – at the creature he mistakes for a butterfly.

As may be clear, this story is not about Mab at all; she is really just a convenient vehicle – a stranger to the land who needs to be guided around, thereby permitting extensive exposition by the Owl. Very little of the former fairy queen remains, except when she hears the music in St Paul's Cathedral, which declares to be like fairyland. Otherwise, she's present mostly to comment on how much things have changed (for the worse): for example, "Mab had found rows on rows of stucco houses, where she had left green fields, running brooks, and hedges white with may, on the northern side of the Strand."[20]

In conclusion, a revolution overwhelms the corrupt British state and Mab decides she had been better off back in the South Seas.

"But Queen Mab... was fain to depart from Britain and renounce the higher civilisation. In the councils of the New Democracy she had no place. Church and State abjured her: the rising generation needed no fairies, but was content with football and cricket, 'Treasure Island,' and the Latin Grammar. Education, Philosophy, and the Philistines had made of the island she once loved well a wilderness wherein no fairy might henceforth furl its wings.

19 Chapter 5.
20 Chapter 8.

She said 'good-bye' to the Owl ... and went back to Samoa. But alas! Samoa, like Great Britain, was no longer any place for her. It was annexed: it was evangelised. The natives of it were going to church; they were going to Sunday School; they were going to heaven... they had no time for fairies.

Queen Mab summoned her Court together in despair, and left for one of the Admiralty Islands. There, till the civilisation that dogs the steps of the old folk-lore has driven her thence – with constitutions, and microscopes, and a higher Pantheism that leaves the older Pantheism in the lurch, and other advantages of the nineteenth century – she is secure... till that lagging island too receives its chrism of intellect, and is caught up into the van of time."[21]

Very much like *Titania's Farewell, That Very Mab* ends on a resigned and regretful note, lamenting the passing of a merry, rural England free of pollution, greed and selfishness. However, as previous chapters have indicated, all was not in fact lost, despite the pessimism late Victorians might have felt about the fate of British fairy-lore. Mab, and all the other famous fairies described in this book, have remained alive in our culture – changed, and changing, perhaps, but very far from forgotten. The contraposition created in these late Victorian books between the neglect and pillaging of the natural world and the fairies has gained new relevance for us today. Likewise, society has rediscovered the need for myth, finding that rationalism and materialism alone did not seem enough.

---

21 Chapter 12.

CHAPTER FOUR

Titania

Titania the fairy queen is not a native British monarch. Her origins are both literary and continental and she was a late arrival at the faery court. Despite this, for many of us today, Titania has become the archetype of the fairy queen, if not of female fairies as a class.

Titania's origins as a fairy queen seem to be Elizabethan. In 1590 Edmund Spenser made his *Faerie Queen* a descendant of Titania, but the character was most explicitly and effectively introduced into fairy-lore by William Shakespeare in *Midsummer Night's Dream*. She was not a traditional character of British folklore (as her name might, in any case, suggest) and the playwright was certainly very well aware of the British equivalent: Queen Mab features prominently in a famous speech by Mercutio in *Romeo and Juliet*, which was first performed in 1597 (see earlier). The *Dream* was written in 1605; did Shakespeare merely want a bit of variety or did he have other motives for creating a new faery monarch?

DIANA

The use of classical names and terms as alternative ways of referring to characters from traditional British folklore was by no means an innovation by Shakespeare. Chaucer, for example, demonstrated his own learning by several times calling his fairy queen Proserpina – and the fairy king Pluto. As the influence of the Renaissance spread, such instances became even more common.[1]

Somewhat like the name of her consort Oberon (see later), Titania's name is more descriptive than personal. 'Titania'

---

1 See too my *Fayerie*, 2020.

simply means that she is born of Titans – though this naturally begs some very important questions. Roman writer Ovid tells us in *The Metamorphoses* that Titania is another name for or aspect of the goddess Diana: he described how she was accidentally seen by a young man when bathing with her nymphs: "while the Titanian Goddess was there bathing in the wonted stream..."[2]

Diana was the Roman deity responsible for childbirth and, as such, there are some significant parallels with Queen Mab the midwife. The Romans also linked Diana to the Greek goddess Artemis, who was primarily a goddess of nature, particularly of springs and water courses. She was, for example, known as Limnaia, 'lady of the lake', a name which for us now is freighted with resonances of Morgan le Fay and other fay maidens and such like nymphs. In her guise as goddess of woods and water, Artemis had obvious parallels with native nature spirits as well as associations with naiads and dryads, who were themselves compared to British fairies. The identification of Diana/Artemis with a British nature goddess or fairy monarch makes considerable sense.

Much more recently in Tudor times, Diana had emerged as the Queen of the witches – as recorded in Reginald Scot's *Discoverie of Witchcraft* of 1584 – and there is evidence that her name was in popular use in this connection in Scotland during the same period. Meanwhile, sixteenth century English and Scots translations of Ovid had made his work much more accessible to readers in the British Isles.[3] Under other epithets, Diana had already been used as a supernatural queen by other poets – for example, Spenser's Belphoebe in *The Faerie Queen* and John Lyly's Cynthia, the moon queen in *Endimion*.[4]

However, Shakespeare had already used the name 'Diana' for a character in *All's Well that Ends Well*, five years previously to *The Dream*, so perhaps again he merely sought variety – or had pursued her mythical links more deeply. Given that Arthur Goulding had used the phrase 'Titan's daughter' in his

---

2 Ovid, Book III, line 173.

3 See for example Gavin Douglas' version in 1513 or Arthur Golding's of 1565.

4 Spenser, *A Letter to Authors*; Lyly, *Endimion*, IV, 3.

translation of Ovid, it could well be possible that the playwright's imagination had been fired and that he had undertaken his own research on her origins and affinities.

DAUGHTER OF TITANS

As I have explained, Diana was descended from the Titans, a heritage which takes us back to the very earliest roots of Greek mythology. The Titans were a race of giants born of Uranus and Ge (heaven and earth). Amongst their numbers were the male gods Oceanus, Cronus, Hyperion, Prometheus and Atlas; amongst the goddesses were numbered Thea, Phoebe and Rhea. The inter-relationships and identities of these beings are far from fixed in the myths, but we need not be too concerned with the details. It is the general tenor of the stories that's significant: they contain a variety of fruitful themes and concepts.

Cronus is often seen as the chief of the Titans. He led a revolt against Zeus and the Olympian gods and was defeated and displaced, being banished with all his kind to imprisonment in Tartarus. It's said that Cronus now sleeps eternally on some western island, and in this respect his myth is very likely to have contributed to the growth of the story of King Arthur sleeping in Avalon. The sister of Cronus was Rhea, but she was also his wife and so mother of a pantheon including Zeus, Poseidon, Hera and others. In this role as divine mother, Rhea is commonly identified with another goddess, Cybele, who was herself worshipped across the ancient world as the Great Mother Goddess. She is another deity of nature, fertility and of wild places and, as such, was fairly readily linked to a fairy queen of groves and springs.

The daughter of the famous Titan Atlas was the equally well-known Calypso, nymph of the island of Ogygia. It was she who detained Odysseus for the magically significant period of seven years and who tried to prevent him ever returning to his wife and home with promises of a grant of immortality. Both the time-scale and the reward must trigger for us thoughts of the detention of mortals in the British fairyland.

In summary, then, these divine female Titans all have attributes and rich associations which provoke thoughts of British equivalents and which tie local beings into a wider and more powerful mythology. It may be for these dramatic reasons that Shakespeare chose the name Titania: she brought with her connotations of power and of antiquity.

SHAKESPEARE'S FAIRY QUEEN

Although she was something of an alien import in name, the Titania of *Midsummer Night's Dream* nevertheless embodied many of the primary aspects of the fairy of British folk tradition.

The amorous interlude with Bottom, played as it is for comedic effect, still incorporates one of the main characteristics of British fairy females. They were drawn inexorably towards human males, acting often as succubi who visited and seduced them at night. This could lead to long-term abduction of the human partners, but it might also prove fatal. Whether in the guise of a mermaid, the Manx *lhiannan shee* or Highland *leanan sithe*, the fairy woman's obsessive love could kill – if only by detaining the human in Faery for so long that the world changed utterly and his earthly body became ancient when he eventually returned.

Next, at the heart of Shakespeare's play is a quarrel between the queen and her consort over a 'little changeling boy.' In fact, this child is not a true fairy changeling – in the sense of a human baby stolen from its parents – but is rather the orphaned son of one of Titania's entourage. Although early in the play Puck states that the boy was "stol'n from an Indian king" the truth is that the mother died during his birth (because she was a mortal) and it is for her sake that the queen is now raising the child. Oberon wants this "lovely boy" and "sweet changeling" to join his followers – which Titania refuses to allow. These details aside, the desire of fairykind for the company of human children is accurate and situates the play's queen firmly within the customary behaviour and attitudes of the fairies of British tradition.

Thirdly, and rather like Artemis / Diana, Shakespeare's fairy queen is intimately associated with the natural environment. Her quarrel with Oberon not only damages their marriage and disturbs the harmony of their court; it disrupts the weather and the growing of the crops. This is summarised by Titania when she tells Bottom that:

> "I am a spirit of no common rate.
> The summer still doth tend upon my state."[5]

She rules over the seasons and they follow her moods.

This new queen therefore inherited much of the wanton sexuality of fairies generally, and especially that of Queen Mab, giving us the erotically tinged imagery of Fuseli and Simmons that will be discussed shortly. The buxom wenches of those paintings are ironic given the fact that Artemis, one of Titania's forms, was also known as a goddess of chastity who was in conflict with Aphrodite (who, in fact, is also of Titan ancestry). Her name may have a classical origin, but Titania's personality is wholly British.

TITANIA AFTER SHAKESPEARE

In due course, the invented character of Titania took on a life of her own, but it was a slow process. The name was taken up by Thomas Dekker in his play *The Whore of Babylon* in 1607, but he was a very early and isolated imitator. Given that the name Titania was such an innovation, and that she was being expected to rival the well-established and well-beloved Queen Mab, it is probably unsurprising to discover that, to begin with, this new character was scarcely mentioned by other playwrights – whether those of Shakespeare's time or during the following century. She may well have seemed too much Shakespeare's own for other writers to have borrowed her, with the result that one of the few other allusions to her seems to have been the fairy

---

5 Act III, scene 1.

named Tita whose wedding is celebrated in the 'Eighth Nimphal' of Michael Drayton's *Muse's Elizium*, which was published in 1630. It may also be more than coincidence that in the play *Amyntas* by Thomas Randolph, the fairies speak a language composed of the syllables 'ti-ta.' Whether this was intended as homage or mockery is not clear.

It was only with the passage of time that Titania became familiar to people through the growing popularity of *Midsummer Night's Dream* – both in stage performances and representations by painters and illustrators. As a consequence, it was not until the nineteenth century that the queen was accepted as one of the rightful members of the fairy court.[6] For example, poet Thomas Hood published *The Plea of the Midsummer Fairies* in 1827. In this, Titania reigns in Faery, but she and all her train are very small: having been compared to a "queen bee," at the very close of the poem she flies away with all "her little crowd / Like flocking linnets, vanish'd in a cloud."[7]

To a very considerable extent, Titania's rise to hegemony in fairyland was a direct reflection of the popularity of *Midsummer Night's Dream* on the stage. After the reign of Charles II, the play was not performed in its entirety until the mid-nineteenth century. This seems to have reflected audience opinion at the time: Samuel Pepys, for instance, attended a performance in September 1662 and dismissed it as "the most insipid, ridiculous play that ever I saw …"

Thereafter, for nearly two centuries, the play was performed only in heavily adapted forms. Composer Henry Purcell based his 1692 masque *The Fairy Queen* very loosely upon it. The Pyramus and Thisbe scenes were excised by Richard Leveridge to create a burlesque opera that was staged in 1716 and 1745. David Garrick got rid of Bottom and the other 'rude mechanicals' for a version titled *The Fairies* in 1755. Another operatic version appeared in 1816.

---

6 See too John Keats, *Sonnet V, To a Friend*, or Francis Noel Clarke Munday, *The Fall of Needwood*, 1830.

7 Robert Henry Forster (1867–1923) dressed Titania in a dress of petals in *Wallflowers*.

It was only in 1840 that audiences once again got to see nearly the whole text as it had been written, when the actress Lucia Vestris produced the play at Covent Garden – albeit including added musical sequences and ballet. Such was the success of this production that Victorian theatres were thereafter encouraged regularly to put on the *Dream* as a spectacular. It has become a firm favourite with the public ever since, not only on the stage but on film and television too. Productions such as those featuring Helen Mirren and Judi Dench (1969), Rupert Everett and Michelle Pfeiffer (1999), or Maxine Peak, John Hannah and Matt Lucas (2016) have repeatedly renewed our affection and refreshed our familiarity with the characters.

At the same time that performances were revived, painters of the nineteenth century enthusiastically seized the opportunities that Titania and her attendants offered to paint classically-inspired life studies (in other words, nude girls). The stage had been set by Henry Fuseli's *Titania and Bottom* and *Titania's Awakening*, both dating to the decade 1780–90, and *Titania, Bottom and the Fairies*, of 1793, which all delighted in gyrating, erotic and sometimes grotesque fairies. In each of the three scenes, the queen is surrounded by courtiers of varying sizes and in various states of undress; some are deformed and ugly, some are seductive. Fuseli established early, therefore, the connection between Faery and naked and unashamedly sexualised females. That said, his *Titania Finds the Magic Ring on the Beach* (1804–5) is a little different. His queen is a classical figure swathed in billowing draperies as she descends head first from the sky. She wears a crescent moon diadem, indicating her affinity with Diana, and she has dragonfly wings, confirming her more conventional fairy nature.

In contrast to Fuseli, Francis Danby, painting in 1832, offered something a little more restrained. His *Scene from Midsummer Night's Dream* is a moonlit grouping of lightly draped and very tiny fairies, with Oberon approaching Titania, who holds a glowing wand taller than she is. His *Oberon and Titania* of 1837 is an almost identical scene, save for the fact that it is set in daylight.

Victorian artists very happily followed these examples. Amongst these are John Lamb's *Midsummer Night's Dream* (1834), Sir Joseph Noel Paton's *Reconciliation of Oberon and Titania* (1847) and the *Quarrel of Oberon and Titania* (1849), Richard Dadd's *Titania Sleeping* (1841) and *Contradiction: Oberon and Titania* of 1854–58, Robert Huskisson's *Midsummer Night's Fairies* (1847) and John George Naish's *Titania Asleep* (1856). All of these paintings show a nude Titania, frequently accompanied by Oberon, and always surrounded by hosts of naked and cavorting faes. Several even more explicitly erotic pictures were painted by John Simmonds, who homed in on the queen's voluptuous naked body; these include *Titania* of 1866, *Titania Flying* (c.1866) and *There Sleeps Titania* (1872). Sir Edwin Landseer's *Titania and Bottom* (1851) is curiously respectable in contrast, his fairy queen being almost fully covered by a classical robe. The same is true of John Anster Fitzgerald's *Titania and Bottom* and *Titania and the Changeling Child*, both of which are undated. This artist always painted his fairies fully clothed in elaborate flower like dresses and headgear. They are both demure and delicate.

The twentieth century began with an apparent move away from nudity. Frank Cadogan Cowper's *When Titania Sleeps* of 1928 shows the queen slumbering on a woodland bank, covered by a rich fabric and surrounded by flowers – poppies, foxgloves and wild-thyme – and watched over by an owl and a rabbit.[8] This may seem a very late example of artistic interest in the play, but we should not forget that Arthur Rackham's still highly popular illustrations to the play were published in 1930. These famed pictures have been very influential upon succeeding generations. His queen and her king are noble and handsome beings, surrounded by hosts of smaller fairies that are either pretty girls or young children with wings – or else elves, whom he depicts as ugly little goblins.

The most recent depiction of the queen is an evolving painting by Peter Blake. His *Titania* is a young female, entirely

---

8   See *Midsummer Night's Dream*, Act II, scene 1.

naked and somewhat feral, her body decorated with objects she has found discarded in our contemporary rural landscape. She has knotted grass stalks around her nipples and has plaited her pubic hair, from which beads are suspended. This Titania is very different from the statuesque and rather coy pin-ups imagined by John Simmons but, for all that, she is still surrounded by a swirl of shadowy, naked girl fairies, just as in the canvases of Paton and his imitators.

The new fairy queen also appeared in a succession of Victorian and early twentieth century verse, including Felicia Hemans' *Fairies' Recall* (1834), Madison Julius Cawein's *On Midsummer Night* (1907), Fenton Johnson's *Eulogy on the Fairies* (1915), Arthur Peterson's *Halloween* (1916) and the *Fairies' Fair* by Zora Bernice May Cross.[9] The continuing influence of Shakespeare was apparently strong, with (for example) two authors retaining the allusions to Midsummer. Reflecting her origin in 'a wood near Athens,' Titania is consistently located by these poems in groves and glades, with insects often acting as her attendants.[10] One of the most striking references to the queen is in *A Fairy Tale*, by English poet Philip James Bailey (1816–1902). She appears there with her consort Oberon and is described memorably as "divine Titania, night's incomparable queen." Even Titania's typical fairy habit of stealing children was recalled and preserved. In his poem *Silvia*, in which he laments the loss of a little girl, Don Marquis (1878–1937) comforted himself with the thought that not death, but the fairies, had taken her:

> "The fairies stole and hold her where
> Death enters not, nor strife nor pain;
> That, drowsing on some bed of pansies,
> By Titania's necromancies
> Her senses were to slumber lulled,

9 See too Peter John Allan, *To Titania, Queen of Fairyland, St Valentine's Day*.

10 For example, William Lisle Bowles (1762–1850), *Fairy Sketch – Scene: Netley Abbey*; Madison Cawein, *Moths & Fireflies* and *Morning Glories*; John Keats, *To Charles Cowden Clarke*; Barcroft Brake (1866–92), *Box Tree's Love*.

Deeply sunken, steeped and dulled,
And by wafture of swift pinions
She was borne out through earth's portals
To the fairy queen's dominions,
To some land of the immortals."

Marquis' vision of Faery is a place that sounds very much like heaven and his fairies' wings are feathered, making them more like angels than mischievous spirits.

For some, of course, Titania and all her court were just poetic names that invoked fond memories of childhood but which no longer had a place in a modern industrialised and scientific world. For Alaric Alexander Watts (1797–1864), for example, fairy tales had become nothing but "beautiful fictions of our trusting youth" and:

"... the bright realm of Fairyland is gone;
Its Iris-tinted train hath passed away;
And Ariel, Mab, Titania, Oberon,
But grace the painter's scene, or poet's lay!
Even Puck, dear imp of mischief and of mirth,
'O'er hill and dale,' at length, hath ceased to range;"

Even so, he concluded that the poet's "heart's home be still in Fairyland!" These famous fairies' names were still the stuff of dreams and the source of inspiration, even to a more 'enlightened' age.[11]

The Victorian period was one during which old beliefs and lifestyles seemed to be under terminal assault. This bred something of a resigned nostalgia for folk tales in many quarters, arising from a regretful but helpless sense that their time was passing away. This mood is exemplified by a curious – and rather slight – short story, *Titania's Farewell*, by Walter Besant and James Rice. It was initially published in the magazine *Once*

---

11 Watts, *A Lament for Fairies*; see too Charles Lamb, *The Fairy*, Mathilde Blind, *Cleve Woods*, or Fenton Johnson, *Dream Song*.

a Week at Christmas 1870 and its sentimental, moralistic and jingoistic tone seem very suited to a family entertainment at that season. The piece subsequently re-appeared in a collection, *The Case of Mr Lucraft and Other Stories,* published in 1878.

As the title suggests, *Titania's Farewell* is concerned with the fairies' departure from England. The events all take place between midnight on Midsummer's Eve and sunrise the next morning. The narrator is staying in the New Forest for a short holiday and gets lost whilst out walking one evening. He resigns himself to sleeping under an oak tree but awakes as a village church clock tolls twelve to discover that he has been bound, hand and foot, and cannot move. He hears music and the fairy court arrives, headed by Titania, Oberon, Mab, Ariel and Puck (who's also called Jack o' Lantern, Robin Goodfellow or Will of the Wisp). The latter whispers to the human to stay still, and quiet, and he will come to no harm. True to tradition, Puck is a mutable prankster: his "face and form changed every moment" and "a mocking light was in his eye, laughter flickered on his lips. He shifted from one form to another; but one knew him always by his eye, unlike any of the rest."

Oberon looks serious, which is because the time has come to leave England forever and to travel to an island in the Indian Ocean. "But three short hours," the king announces, "but three short hours, and the kingdom of Faerie will be over in Merry England – merry, alas! no more." He continues:[12]

> "We have known and loved it so well: we have blessed so many mansions, dropped a charm over so many cottages, spread love and tenderness over so many homes, danced in so many woods, lived in so many haunts; and now we must go!... There is no land like the land of the English – no forests like theirs, no lawns like their lawns. We love not the rank grass and the heavy-flowering trees of the tropics; the crested palm is not like the leafy elm; the scent of spices is not to us like the perfume of the wild thyme and the

---

12 1878 edition, 134.

primrose. We love not the black man so well as the Saxon. Their children have been our playthings, their maidens our care; their singers have been taught by us; their children's games are ours; their joys are our joys. And they forget us – they forget us!"

Once the English had loved the fairies, and relied upon their help, Oberon laments, but they no longer believe in them, a fact he blames upon the Education Act and the School Boards: "Now, all is changed. The song is no more of Robin Goodfellow and the Brownies: they tell of the poor man's suffering, the rich man's luxury. The folk are more wealthy than they were, but they are not so contented. The new songs which the poets sing are of the earth, earthy. It is time that we go."

Various other supernatural beings then appear, asking to be allowed to go with the fairies because they too are neglected and forgotten. Only the gnomes and Puck's friend Number Nip the mountain spirit allowed to accompany the court; the banshee, bogey, wraiths and others are refused.[13] The fairies then reflect regretfully on their past exploits – how they helped true lovers and abducted musicians to play at their dances – following which Puck and Queen Mab lament their current plights. Puck had been known and loved by all as Robin Goodfellow or the brownie – "I was their friend, though I played them a thousand pranks. They speak of me no more – I am forgotten." Rationality has left no space for him. Mab, meanwhile, has continued to try to bring hope and relief to people in their dreams. Now, however she must sadly admit that her role is redundant: she says to Titania, "Take my sceptre and my crown, for I am no longer Queen of Dreams."

Turning to Titania herself, she had tried to bring poetry and joy into the lives of the English people, but the queen is driven to admit that fairy poetry had disappeared from England ever since the death of Thomas Hood.

---

13 Number-Nip, also called Rubezahl, is a Germanic sprite whose story was made familiar by the Grimm Brothers. As we'll see a little later, he also featured in an opera with King Oberon.

"They believe in us no more," said the King. "We were associated with things beautiful, things weird, things kindly; but all things pass away, and we with them."

"After all," said Puck, "it would be very unpleasant for us to stay here, even if they did believe in us. The smoke of the factories poisons us; there are hardly any forests where we can lurk; no rivers but are foul with refuse; hardly any commons but are enclosed by the Lord of the Manor. They've stolen great slices of Epping Forest, and wanted to build over Hampstead Heath; and on the sea-shore are the Coast-guard."

"It is the worse for them," said Oberon. "Woe to those whom the fairies love not! ... Their hearts will only grow harder when we have left the land. Knowledge will come without Wisdom, Riches without Content, Power without Greatness, and everything without Love."

"It will be the worse for the children," said Titania. "They will lose all the pretty legends which made life a romance to them. Why should they learn hard things? Why should they be taught the lesson of utility, in this iron age, so soon? Why should they not, like the brave men of old, be taught to cherish the memories of the good people? They are little chemists now, and little philosophers; little linguists, little scorners and scoffers at what they cannot understand."[14]

Then, with the dawn, the fairies vanish. All that remains is a fairy ring, created by many tiny feet. The king and queen's coach has become a dry leaf; her globe is an acorn, her sceptre a reed; Oberon's crown is nothing but a wreath of wild flowers and Mab's wand is just a twig. The narrator concludes:

"Not altogether vain," I thought, "was the cult of the fairies – not a superstition that brought evil with it – a relic of Paganism touched with the light of the new religion, something to help us sometimes to shake off reality, and live in the ideal."

14 1878 edition, 172.

Despite this effort to sound optimistic, the late Victorian might have been justified in thinking that fairy belief had entered an irreversible decline in the face of materialism and 'progress.' Against all expectation, however, Titania and her followers enjoyed a spectacular revival during the twentieth century. The Cottingley fairy photographs are but one instance of this, but that incident was reflective of a deeper need for mystery and wonder within a Western society no longer sure of its inexorable advance towards improvement and comfort.

As the source of dreams and reassurance, the fairy queen could even manifest herself to a poet amidst the carnage and destruction of the First World War, as in Edmund Blunden's *Premature Rejoicing,* set near the shattered Thiepval Wood, part of the Somme battlefield of 1916. He is examining the scene of recent fighting through binoculars:

> "There sleeps Titania (correct – the Wood is ours);
> There sleeps Titania in a deep dugout,
> Waking, she wonders what all the din's about,
> And smiles through her tears, and looks ahead ten years,
> And sees the Wood again, and her usual Grenadiers,
>
> All in green,
> Music in the moon;
>
> The burnt rubbish you've just seen
> Won't beat the Fairy Queen;"

It was against the same background of hope that Robert Graves composed his poem *Babylon,* in which he suggests the struggle to retain his belief in Oberon and Puck in the face of wisdom and reality, which – he lamented – had battered Babylon all to bits.[15]

---

15 Graves, *Fusiliers and Fairies,* 1918.

CHAPTER FIVE

Other Faery Queens & Women

"I fell asleep and dreamed of fairyland…
A blue-haired fairy took me by the hand
And med me towards a palace where a band
Of fays, with locks like pink fronds that rise
Within the sea-waves, danced in gleesome wise:
Then came the fairy queen with golden wand.
She moved to meet me. When my eyes met hers,
I felt along my veins a sudden thrill,
As when the passionate young blood leaps and stirs:
I woke: I lay upon a low sand hill…
But that queen's hazel glances haunt me still."[1]

This verse by George Barlow is quite an erotic fantasy. The coloured hair may seem slightly less exotic than it did in 1890, but it still carries an implication of punk rebellion and a mild fetish thrill, whilst the fairy queen herself embodies entirely the powerful sexuality that has always been associated with faery women – and most especially faery royalty (as epitomised by the queens of *Thomas of Erceldoune* and *Sir Launfal*, who provoke their mortal male lovers into feats of sustained intercourse).

Besides the famous faery queens we have just examined, a considerable number of other monarchs are known, some of whom are named and others of whom are anonymous. The sixteenth century Scottish poet Montgomerie wrote of "the King of Pharie with the court of the Elph-quene" and in the nineteenth

---

1   George Barlow, 'Fairy Land,' sonnet VII in *Miscellaneous Poems from Dawn to Sunset*, 1890.

century the poet William Aytoun set out the typical Presbyterian view when he stated that "The queen of fairyland was a kind of feudatory sovereign under Satan, to whom she was obliged to pay kane or tithe in kind [that is, in human souls]." A similar anonymous queen plays a central role in the ballad of *Tam Lin*.[2]

Scottish witchcraft suspect Isobel Gowdie claimed that she had been favoured with gifts of meat (food) by the 'Qwein of Fearrie' who was "brawlie clothed in whyt linens, and white and browne cloathes." This queen had a partner, an anonymous king, as was the case too with the faery queen of the ballad of *Thomas of Erceldoune* – and from whom her sexual relationship with mortal Thomas had to be concealed.[3]

Accused witch Isobel Watson was privileged enough to be midwife to an unnamed fairy queen, whereas Alison Pearson, from St Andrews in Fife, failed to achieve such intimate access. She had (deceased) relatives who resided in the fairy court and who were on good terms with the queen, she told to her trial in 1588, but she personally had never met her majesty, who was, by all accounts, quite a moody individual. Sometimes she was good, sometimes evil; sometimes she was present in the court and sometimes elsewhere.[4] Another anonymous queen was met by Andro Man of Aberdeen – who entered into a long-term sexual relationship with her and was taught healing and prophetic skills by her. Elizabeth Dunlop from Lyne near Peebles was endowed with the same knowledge by the queen herself.[5]

Alleged witch Bessie Dunlop was visited in her own home by the queen, who looked to her like any ordinary middle-aged woman, stout and in need of a glass of beer. The most extreme example of the ordinariness of fairy queens is probably the story of Angus Mór of Tomnahurich, in which the nameless queen is

---

2 Montgomerie, *Flyting Between Montgomerie & Polwart*, 1515 (and see too Lyndesay, *Complaynt of the Papago*); Aytoun cited in Simpson, *Folklore in Lowland Scotland*, 97.

3 Pitcairn, *Ancient Criminal Trials in Scotland*, vol.3, Part 2, 602.

4 Stirling Presbytery Records, CH2/722/2 (1590); Pitcairn, *Ancient Criminal Trials in Scotland*, vol.1, Part 3, 161.

5 *Spalding Club Miscellany*, vol.1, Part 3, 120.

encountered doing her washing on a rock in a stream. A tale from Lochranza on the Isle of Arran, features a fairy queen who's seen in a harvest field in the shape of a large pregnant yellow frog. These monarchs were evidently not proud individuals, too regal to lift a finger.[6]

In addition to these plentiful Scottish examples, there is the story of the 'white powder' from the East Riding of Yorkshire. A man received a healing powder from the fairy queen, whom he met in her court under a small hill. There she was to be found "sitting in great state and many people about her." Despite him being an illiterate, poor man, she made him welcome and assisted him to make a living by being able to cure the sick. As with many of the preceding examples, faery monarchs don't seem to object to dealing with the humblest of mortals – perhaps they can't tell the differences in status between humans.[7]

Fascinatingly, Janet Boyman, a healer from Edinburgh who was tried for witchcraft in 1572, used to invoke both God and the faeries to give efficacy to her cures. Her treatments involved calling upon "the father, the son, King Arthur and Queen Elspeth." We'll discuss Arthur again a little later, whilst Elspeth is otherwise unknown. The sixteenth century love charms mentioned in the first chapter also invoked Jesus, the holy trinity and the king and queen of Faery to assist in summoning faery helpers.[8]

To summarise, the apparent multiplicity of queens that this introduction reveals would appear to imply that witnesses accepted that there were numerous faery kingdoms, each with its own monarch. The rulers usually weren't named, probably because they are seen as one amongst many. The names derived from literature – Titania and, to some extent, Mab- weren't used because – it would seem- they were known not to be relevant to queens ruling in the real world. This idea of multiple monarchies

---

6 Pitcairn, *Ancient Criminal Trials*, vol.1, 49–58; MacDougall & Calder, *Folk Tales & Fairy Lore*, 133; Robertson, 'Folklore from the West of Ross-shire,' *Transactions of the Gaelic Society of Inverness*, vol.26, 1905, 271.

7 Gutch, *County Folklore, East Riding*, vol.6, 55; Webster, *The Displaying of Supposed Witchcraft*, 300–302.

8 Sloane 3850, ff.145–166.

was taken up again in the twentieth century by author Sylvia Townsend Warner, who envisaged a patchwork of kingdoms across Britain.[9]

GWENHIDW

Many readers will be familiar with *The Fairy Faith in Celtic Countries*, by Walter Evans-Wentz. They might even recall that, in his investigation of Welsh fairy lore, he spoke to a Welsh Justice of the Peace from Carmarthen called David Williams, who proved a rich source of faery facts, despite his sober and respectable position. In particular, he told Evans-Wentz about the king and queen of the *tylwyth teg*, whom he named as Gwydion ab Don and his wife Gwenhidw. Gwydion is a character straight out of the *Mabinogion*, and he is said to live amongst the stars in Caer Gwydion, one of several magical faery fortresses that are mentioned in Welsh legend. His wife, meanwhile, is connected to the fluffy white clouds that appear in fine weather and which are called 'the sheep of Gwenhidw.'

This is a very pretty image, and Evans-Wentz goes on to speculate that this queen has some connection to King Arthur's queen Guinevere, who is more properly Gwenhwyfar, 'the white ghost' or spirit. Ghostly 'white ladies' are very common in British folklore, of course, often associated with wells and streams.[10]

Mr David Williams JP gave Evans-Wentz a very useful lead, but what he had learned as a boy from his mother was a very confused version of the authentic tradition. Gwenhidw (or Gwenhidwy/Gwenhudwy) is well known in Welsh folklore. She is, actually, a *morforwyn* – a mermaid. Her name means 'white enchantment' or 'white spell.' In modern stories she owns a herd of white horses that run along the crests of the waves. In older versions of the tale, the foaming waves were her ewes and every ninth wave was the ram of the flock. This conception of the incoming tide is preserved in a sixteenth century poem by

---

9   See Warner, *Kingdoms of Elfin*, 1977 & *Of Cats & Elfins*, 2020.
10 See my *Beyond Faery*, 2020.

Rhys Llywd ap Rhys ap Rhicert in which he described a boat trip to the monastic island of Bardsey (Ynys Enlli) from the Lleyn Peninsula. The passage is notoriously choppy and he described the sea as:

"*haid o ddefaid Gwenhudwy/ a naw hwrdd yn un a hwy*"
(a flock of ewes of Gwenhidwy and nine rams with them.)

Another poem of a comparably early date refers to Gwenhidw growing a beard (*Ni adaf mal Gwenhudwy/ Ar vy min dyfu barf mwy* – "Like G., I no longer grow a beard on my lip.") This seems to be an example of the quite widespread British tradition that mermaids are (contrary to popular misconceptions) pretty unattractive to look at – and possibly not even very different to tell from mermen.

Elsewhere in Welsh tradition a flood is termed 'Gwenhudwy's oppression' and the sea is called her 'plain.' Lastly, an Elizabethan poem contrasts a man called Rhys Cain to our heroine, saying that he is a 'feeble magician' compared to her (*wan hydol i Wenhidw*).

What can we conclude from these scattered references? It emerges that Gwenhidw was once well-known in Wales as a powerful and fearsome mermaid, someone to be dreaded and respected. If insulted, her vengeance might be savage.

Figuratively, at least, Gwenhidw had flocks of sheep. At some point (though perhaps only in the family of David Williams JP) a misconception arose and the rolling breakers of the angry sea were substituted by benign fair-weather clouds. This, along with her marriage to Gwydion, demoted Gwenhidw, but she deserves to be restored to her far more prominent position as sorceress and queen.

GYRE-CARLING

In the East of Scotland, especially in Fife, the spirit known as the *gyre-carlin* (or gy-carling and variants thereon), was a female faery who was particularly linked to cloth-making. It was said that, if unspun flax was not removed from the distaff at the end of the year, she would steal it all. Conversely, if asked by a woman for the endowment of skill in spinning, the gyre carling would enable the recipient to do three to four times as much work as other spinners. Despite these humble domestic aspects, though, the *gyre-carlin* had a more fearsome side to her character. She was the Lowland equivalent of the *cailleach*, or hag, being well-armed, violent and partially cannibalistic. Perhaps for this reason, she was also called *Nicnevin* (see next section).[11]

A satirical poem of 1584 by Robert Sempill attacked the bishop of St Andrews in Fife for having used the services of a healer called Alison Pearson to treat various ailments. She was later convicted as a witch, with clear reputational repercussions for the bishop.[12] Sempill described at one point how:

> "Ane carling of the Quene of Phareis,
> That ewill win geir to elphyne careis;
> Through all Braid Abane scho hes bene,
> On horsbak on Hallow ewin;
> And ay in seiking certayne nyghtis,
> As scho sayis, with sur sillie wychtis…"

This servant of the fairy queen is a 'carline' or 'carling' – a stout and bad-tempered woman and (by extension) a witch. She is seen riding out at Halloween across 'Albany' (Scotland) with her loyal "sillie wychtis," making it virtually certain that these 'seelie wights' are other members of this faery queen's court.

The carline's association with the last faery rade of the year at Halloween was widespread. Recording the folk belief of Dumfries and Galloway, Robert Cromek described her in this connection as "the mother of glamour, and near akin to Satan himself. She is believed to preside over the ' Hallowmass Rades,'

---

11 *County Folklore*, vol.7, 34; Mackenzie, *Scottish Folk Lore*, c.VII.
12 Sempill, *Heir Followis the Legend of the Bishop of St. Androis Lyfe, Callit Mr. Patrick Adamsone, Alias Cousteane*, 1584.

and mothers frequently frighten their children by threatening to give them to M'Neven, or the Gyre Carline. She is described as wearing a long grey mantle, and carrying a wand, which, like the miraculous rod of Moses, could convert water into rocks, and sea into solid land."[13]

The word 'carling' that Sempill uses entered Northern Middle English (and Scots) from Old Norse *kerling*. The related word in southern English is 'churl' (directly from the Anglo-Saxon *ceorl* with only a minor vowel change). The hard initial consonant of 'carline' indicates the word's Norse source – and might even imply an origin in the far north, in the Viking kingdom of Orkney and Shetland. One proposed derivation of the word is certainly from Orkney, combining *gygr* (giantess) with *karlinna/kerling*, meaning an old woman – hence a 'crone' or 'hag.'[14]

In this giant guise, the carline appears in a Scots poem found in the Bannatyne manuscript. 'The Gyre Carling' tells that she lived in a tower at Beattock, near Moffat, and ate the flesh of humans. She had a club of iron to defend herself – which she needed when she was besieged by the "king of fary" who came "with elffis mony ane" (with many elves). She fled from him and his pack of hounds (all the dogs from Dunbar to Dunblane, apparently) by taking getting astride a pig: she "schup her on ane sow and is her gaitis gane" (she settled herself on a sow and went her ways). In David Lyndsay's poem of 1528, *The Dreme,* the 'Gyir Carlyng' appears alongside the three headed giant, the Red Etin, implying that she was of comparably large and scary.

Walter Scott, meanwhile, regarded the *gyre* or *gay carline* as a type of witch. Another Scottish poet, John Leyden, termed her both the mother witch Hecate *and* the queen of fairies. Overall, it seems it's probably safest to assume she's more faery than witch.[15]

---

13 Cromek, *Remains of Nithsdale & Galloway Song*, 1810, 292.
14 Marwick, *Folklore of Orkney & Shetland*, 32; J. Saxby, *Shetland Traditional Lore*, 132–3.
15 Scott, *Minstrelsy of the Scottish Borders*, vol.2, 326; Leyden, *Complaynt of Scotland*, 319.

The gyre carline apparently enjoys the simple entertainment of outdoor sports. It was reported in the late eighteenth century that, during winter nights, "Gyar Carlins" and faeries could be heard curling on frozen lochs. In addition to these benign activities, however, they would stop humans who were out and about at Halloween and stuff them full of butter and beare awns (barley husks); they were also prone to taking children and leaving changelings.[16]

Although many of the places named in association with the gyre-carline are in the south of Scotland, it must also be observed that she was known throughout the country. In Sutherland, in the very north of the mainland, she was, once again, associated with spinning. The carline only appeared twice in the year, at Candlemas (February 2nd) and on Shrove Tuesday, at which seasons she took the form of an old woman (as her name partly implies). If the drive band were not removed from a household's spinning wheel, she would commandeer it and work through the night, making so much noise that the family was woken and then kept awake with fear. Houses had to be prepared in advance of her arrival, most notably setting out a bowl of fresh water so that she could bathe her child, whom she brought with her (a trait which clearly links her with wider faery kind).[17]

NICNEVIN

Nicnevin may well be identical with the Gyre Carling. There are various interpretations of this faery female's name: it may mean 'daughter of heaven' or something like 'daughter of bones.' She has also been linked to the Irish war goddess Badb, who is also called Neamhain; hence, the being is the child of the deity. Other spellings provide alternative derivations, such as NicNaomhin,

---

16 Robert Heron, *Observations on a Journey Through the Western Counties of Scotland*, 1793, vol.2, 228.
17 G. Calder, *Sketches from John O'Groats*, 223–224.

'daughter of the little saint' and NicCreamhain, 'daughter of the little tree man.'[18]

Nicnevin seems, like the gyre, to be a giantess, hence Walter Scott calling her a hag and a "gigantic and malignant female" whom he links to witches (seeing her as cognate with Hecate and Diana) and who rides on storms. A witch from Crieff tried in about 1615 was called Catherine Nevin, reinforcing this association. One authority has suggested that she got her surname from her neighbours because they identified her with the faery queen. The same may well be the case for another 'witch' and folk healer, Margaret NicLevine of Bute, who was tried in 1662. She cured various maladies using charms, rituals and herbs.[19]

The poet Montgomerie describes this female on Halloween riding with a monstrous and evil company of faeries, including the elf king and queen:

"Nicniven, with hir nymphes in number anew [enough],
With chairmes from Caithness and Chanrie of Rosse,
Whais cunning consists in casting a clew...
The king of phairie, and his court, with the elf queine,
With mony elrich incubus was rydand that nycht."[20]

The verse in question is a 'flyting' – a formal ridiculing – of a man called Polwarth. In Montgomerie's account, Polwarth was reared by Nicneven, who taught him all her magical skills – such as sailing across the sea in a sieve and telling the future by examining knotted threads (the 'clew casting' mentioned above).

Early in the last century, the name of Nicnevin was still associated with Faery. A woman from Quarff on Shetland claimed to be acquainted with some local trows among whom were Sara Neven, as well as Robbie a da Rees.[21]

---

18 Mackenzie, *Scottish Folk Lore*, 149–150; M. Daimler, *A New Dictionary of Fairies*, 251.
19 Scott, *Letters on Demonology*, 128–129; C. Sharpe, *A Historical Account of the Belief in Witchcraft in Scotland*, 1880, 159; McPhail, *Highland Papers*, vol.3, 1920, 9.
20 Montgomerie, *The Flyting of Polwart*.
21 Henderson, *Scottish Fairy Belief*, 16.

HABETROT

In the Scottish Lowlands and Border regions, we find the spinner Habetrot, whose bottom lip is distended, misshapen through years of pulling thread. As patron of spinning, Habetrot may be the Selkirkshire version of the Highland *loireag*.[22]

It's possible that Habetrot's name is related in some way to Habundia, a name used by some for the queen of the faeries and witches. As Habonde, she first appeared in a couple of thirteenth century French texts, and she seems ultimately to derive from the Roman goddess *Abundantia*. Suffice to say, it's not a native name, but it may have been combined with the English element 'trot' which is discussed later in the chapter on *Rumpelstiltskin and his Kin*.[23]

Habetrot has a team of helpers, which includes a fae called Scantlie Mab. Just like her mistress, Mab has a drooping lip from a lifetime spent at the spinning wheel, but she's also cursed with bulging eyes and a long, hooked nose. 'Scantly' might be a nickname, implying her small size, as in the dialect word 'scantling.' It may also be worth adding that Thomas Keightley suggested that Mab was derived by Habundia. In essence, therefore, these two names might really just mean Big and Little Mab.[24]

FAERY GODMOTHERS

The idea of the fairy godmother is embedded in our contemporary views of Faery. However, it has been suggested that this female figure is a relatively recent and extraneous introduction to existing tradition, something that was derived

---

22 W. Henderson, *Folklore of the Northern Counties*, 1879, 258-262; also see my *Beyond Faery*, 2020, c.7.

23 See my *British Fairies*, 2017, c.27 & Thomas Keightley, *Fairy Mythology*, 1828, 474-6.

24 Keightley, *Fairy Mythology*, pages 331 footnote & 476 footnote; in the latter he refers to Heywood, *Hierarchie of Blessed Angels*, viii, 517, where he treats Habundia as queen of the white ladies.

from the Brothers Grimm and from stories like *Pinocchio* and *Cinderella*, and has since been reinforced by popular films, rather than it being a long-standing element of folklore belief. In this section I'd like to challenge that idea and to argue instead that it is one of the oldest recognised aspects of faery behaviour.

One of the pastimes or habits of medieval faeries was to either bless or torment humans. According to the historian Layamon, for example, King Arthur was blessed by elves at his birth (this is, by far, our earliest faery godmother account, as the writer was born around 1200). In the thirteenth century French romance, *Huon of Bordeaux*, too, there is a reference to a healing horn that's presented to faery king Oberon by four faery 'godmothers.' Hearing a blast upon it would make the sickest man whole and sound instantly.

The fourteenth century romance of *Ogier the Dane* mixes fairy material with the figures and stories from the 'Matter of Britain,' the legends of King Arthur and the exploits of the knights of the Round Table. At his birth, Ogier is endowed with gifts and qualities by six fairy women; the last of these, Morgana, declares "I claim you as my own. You shall not die until you have visited me in Avalon." After many adventures serving King Charlemagne, Ogier is shipwrecked on a strange island that turns out to be Morgana's realm. He falls under her seductive spell and passes a hundred years in bliss, not ageing a day, until by accident he recovers his memory and wishes to return to France. On doing so, Ogier finds a new king, Hugh Capet, on the throne, whilst the language spoken has changed during his long absence. After more noble deeds, Morgana reclaims Ogier for herself and takes him back to Avalon – where he is still alive today, alongside King Arthur.

Amongst the christening gifts made by faery females is the very famous song of Dunvegan Castle on the Isle of Skye. This was a lullaby, sung over the cradle of the new-born heir to the clan MacLeod by a fairy woman. It foretold the child's strength in arms and that he would possess plenty of cattle and rich crops in the fields; it promised that he would be free from injury in battle and would enjoy a long life. Each verse of the song had a different tune. For many generations afterwards, the custom of the clan was to sing the protective charm over the latest baby heir.

In Tudor times the belief still lingered that some children might be endowed with talents and good fortune at their birth, as in these lines by John Milton (*At a Vacation Exercise in the Colledge*):

> "Good luck befriend thee Son; for at thy birth,
> The Faiery Ladies daunc't upon the hearth;
> Thy drowsie Nurse hath sworn she did them spie
> Come tripping to the Room where thou didst lie;
> And sweetly singing round thy Bed,
> Strew all their blessings on thy sleeping Head…"

These conceptions of course persist for modern readers in the fixed character of the 'fairy godmother,' but in Tudor and Stuart times it seems that the favour of the fairy kingdom was envisaged as being distributed more generally (and generously), as in these lines by Ben Jonson:

> "To what strange fortune, friend, some men are born…
> Surely, when thou wert young,
> The fairies dandled thee."[25]

In Victorian verse the idea of both fairy godmothers and of the grant of three wishes was greatly elaborated, most notably with mermaids, thereby embedding it in our consciousness. See, for example, 'The Fairy Gift,' 'The Fairy and the Three Wishes' and 'The Farmer and the Magic Ring,' all by John Godfrey Saxe; 'The Fairy's Gift,' by Margaret Elizabeth Munson Sangster, in *Poems of the Household* (1893) and 'Wise Sarah and The Elf' by Elizabeth Coatsworth.[26]

---

25 *The Silent Woman*, Act V, scene 1.
26 Generally, see my *Victorian Fairy Verse*.

As the last paragraph indicates, a further and related cliché of faery lore is that the faeries may grant our wishes – often in threes, because this is a magical and significant number (at least in Christian tradition). This idea is – once again – more the substance of fairy-tales and fairy godmothers than authentic British folklore, but it's not entirely without foundation in native accounts.

Mermaids seem especially prone to granting triple wishes. In the Cornish story of Lutey and the mermaid, the maid granted Lutey three wishes as a reward for returning her to the sea after she had become stranded on the beach. The mermaid in the related Cornish story, *The Old Man of Cury,* grants a single wish, as does the Manx mermaid who falls for a man who woos her with gifts of apples.[27]

The fairy women of Scotland seem especially inclined to grant wishes to humans. What's bestowed is often skills – which may be taught, exchanged for sex, or which may be given as rewards. Often, the grant is offered conditionally: the recipient can have either 'ingenuity without advantage' or 'advantage without ingenuity.' One will mean that the one will be clever and highly skilled, but will never be rich; the other will make the man prosperous, but he will be stupid. Abilities in crafts or music are often conferred; even a great skill in thieving can be granted, apparently. On occasion, though, these awards are not really gifts at all, and a price may be exacted, which can even be the eventual forfeit of the human him or herself. This was the case with Lutey, who was eventually abducted by the mermaid he saved; in the Scottish tale of Peter Waters of Caithness, he met a fairy woman at a well and she spontaneously offered to endow him with great prowess, either as a preacher or as a piper. He chose to be a piper and she even gave him a set of pipes. All she asked was that, in return, they meet again after seven years. In the meantime, he won great fame and fortune

---

27 See 'Lutey and the Mermaid' in Bottrell, *Traditions & Hearthside Stories of West Cornwall*, vol.1; S. Morrison, *Manx Fairy Tales*, 71.

for his music but when he duly returned to meet her at the well, he was never seen again.[28]

An unusual Scottish Gaelic story builds upon this general idea. The fairy queen (who is generally identified with the goddess Fann, the embodiment of skill) was grieved by the lack of wisdom amongst many women in the world. She therefore breathed on the fairy flax plant and issued a summons to every woman in the world to come to her knoll to be endowed with wisdom. Many came and the queen appeared before them, carrying a limpet in which there was the *ais* or skill of wisdom. Each woman was invited to drink from the shell, according to her faith and desire. Sadly, the cup ran dry before all could benefit.[29]

In conclusion, faery godmothers and wish granting faeries are a fixture of British tradition, but they are nearly always anonymous.

28 J.G. Campbell, *Superstitions*, 159 & 181.
29 Carmichael, *Carmina Gadelica*, vol.2, 248.

CHAPTER SIX

Oberon

Most readers will be familiar with the name of Oberon as the king of fairyland. William Shakespeare is responsible for this, but he borrowed the name; he did not invent it. It derives from the early to mid-thirteenth century French romance *Huon of Bordeaux*. In that story Oberon/ Auberon appears as a magical fairy king – as well as being a dwarf who's the height of a three-year-old child as the result of an enchantment. A dwarfish fairy king was not a unique notion: the same is true of the fairy king in the English romance of *King Herla*). Auberon is a French name, an affectionate diminutive form of Aubert, which in turn is derived the Frankish/ Germanic name Alberic (to which we may compare the Anglo-Saxon Aelfric) and which means no more than 'elf rule.' In other words, this is not really a name at all, it's just a job title – 'King of the Elves.'

OBERON BEFORE THE *DREAM*

The faery king's name seems to have been familiar to English speakers well before its use by Shakespeare. For example, a very revealing incident concerning the collection of magical fern seed was described by the Puritan preacher Thomas Jackson in 1625:[1]

> "It was my happe since I undertook the Ministrie to question an ignorant soule... what he saw or heard when he watch't the falling of the Ferne-seed at an unseasonable and suspitious houre. Why (quoth he) ... doe you think that the devil hath aught to do with that good seed? No: it is in the keeping of the King of Fayries and he, I know, will do me no harm: yet he had utterly forgotten this King's

---

1 *A Treatise Concerning the Original of Unbelief*, 1625, 178–9.

65

name until I remembered it unto him out of my reading of *Huon of Bordeaux*." (i.e. the king was Oberon)

Whilst extensive literary use was made of the name, it had already penetrated into popular culture. This is clearly shown by two cases in which conjurors had sought to raise spirits on behalf of clients: in 1444 a man was pilloried in London for his attempts to contact 'Oberycom' and in 1510 a Halifax fraudster alleged that he had communicated with 'Oberion.' This same fairy 'Oberion' is found in the grimoire now called *The Book of Oberon*. This collection of practical spells and talismans is dated to about 1577; in it, a procedure is described for the conjuration of the powerful spirit Oberion, who is married to the fairy queen Mycob and has seven daughters. He is illustrated three times in the book; he is twice seen crowned and wielding a sword, whereas in the other picture, he looks very much like a genie emerging from a bottle. It is said of Oberion that "he teacheth a man knowledge in physick, and he showeth the nature of stones, herbs, and trees and of all metal."

The king's consort Mycob (or sometimes Micol) is said to appear dressed in green and is, like her husband, skilled in the use of herbs and medicines. Often invoked alongside her is another spirit who's called Titam. This name is also found written as Titem, Tytarit, Titan, Tytan, Tytar or, even, Setan and Chicam. There's a very wide range of spellings, but this spirit could clearly relate to Titania, discussed in the previous chapter. The name 'Mycob' itself, meanwhile, has been suggested to be a variant of Mab, whom we will examine later.

Given the foregoing evidence of familiarity with Oberon, it's worth noting that a translation of the original French romance in which he featured did not appear until about 1540, when John Bourchier, Lord Berners, published his English version *Huon of Burdeuxe*. This late availability of an accessible text notwithstanding, as we can see, the story already seemed to be very well-known within the general population.

The familiarity of the fairy king's name is further confirmed by the fact that Oberon was recruited as the father of Robin

Good-fellow in a succession of Stuart chapbooks. The fullest version may be found in *Robin Goodfellow – his Mad Prankes and Merry Jests,* which is dated 1628, but which doubtless reproduces established folk stories. Robin is the son of a "proper young Wench." She is visited nightly by a "hee fairy" in her chamber. At first the story is rather circumspect about this male's identity: "whether he was their king or no I know not, but surely he had great government and command in that country, as you shall heare." His status appears to be confirmed by his care for the girl after the son is born:

> "... every night his mother was supplied with necessary things that are befitting a woman in child-birth, and that in no meane manner neither; for there had shee rich imbroidered cushions, stooles, carpits, coverlets, delicate linen; then for meate shee had capons, chickins, mutton, lambe, pheasant, snite, woodcocke, partridge, quaile... wine had shee of all sorts, as muscadine, sacke, malmsie, claret, white and bastard... Sweet meates too had they in such aboundance that some of their teeth are rotten to this day and for musicke shee wanted not, or any other thing shee desired."

Very evidently, this is no ordinary father and, after many adventures and exploits, it is revealed to Robin that his father is, in fact, King Obreon. The king comes to his son with "many fayries, all attired in greene silke" and welcomes him into their company. Obreon confirms his love for his son by taking him to fairyland where he showed him "many secrets, which hee never did open to the world."

The *Ballad of Robin Goodfellow* is a rhymed version of this same life story, but adds a few additional details. From the outset, it admits that it is King Oberon, touring human houses for entertainment at night, who is attracted to the "comely lass." He seduces this "lovely damsel... so courteous, meek and mild" but she does not know his identity. The midwife who attends her son's birth suspects the truth, though, especially when the absent father supplies the new mother with "store of linen... With dainty cates and choised fare / He served her like a lady." Robin learns of his father's true nature when he awakes one day to find a scroll beside him which promises to teach him all his parent's "mysterious skill."[2]

Oberon appeared regularly too in plays, masques and poetry. In Spenser's *Faerie Queen,* published between 1590 and 1596, he was identified with Henry VIII and was described as "mightie;" "Great was his power and glorie over all," Spenser added, flattering the late king's daughter, who by then ruled as Elizabeth I.[3] Robert Greene's *Scottish Historie of James the Fourth* (1594) features 'Oboram, King of Fayeries' as a kind of narrator or master of ceremonies. Despite his royalty, he is the little king of puppet-like subjects, who "look'st not so big as the king of Clubs." In *Lust's Dominion, or The Lascivious Queen,* a collaboration of 1600 between Dekker, Haughton and Day, Oberon has a comparable role. He appears with music and dancing fairies and foretells the fate of the heroine Maria. The fairy king was also seen in William Percy's play *The Faery Pastorall* (1603).

SHAKESPEARE'S OBERON

Midsummer Night's Dream is believed to have been written in 1595–96, but it did not receive its first performance until January 1st 1605. As scholar Floris de Lattre described, the fairy king's status was about to be transformed:

> "Oberon has been removed from the world of romance, where he was still a dwarf, and brought among the tiny Teutonic elves, while Puck, on the other hand, so familiar to every country homestead, appears as Oberon's court jester, being thus put under the fairy king's direct subjection."[4]

---

2 *Ballad*, chapters I & III.
3 *Faerie Queen*, 1590, Book II, c.10, stanzas 75–76.
4 De Lattre, *English Fairy Poetry*, 112.

We shall consider Puck's parallel metamorphosis in due course. Oberon's role in Shakespeare's play is to be 'Captain of the fairy band' and 'King of shadows' but also to be a magician, something akin to Prospero in *The Tempest*. There is, too, a suggestion that he differs in some degree from the rest of the fairies around him. When Puck warns of the imminent dawn, that will drive the spirits away, Oberon replies "we are spirits of another sort," and as such they are able to withstand the sun's rays.[5]

Oberon is portrayed by Shakespeare as unfaithful to his wife, enjoying affairs with humans – if not other fairies – over and above which he is cruelly vengeful, plotting to humiliate his wife by making her fall in love with "lion, bear or wolf, or bull, [or] meddling monkey [or] busy ape." The consequences of this, though, the king appears to regret – and swiftly reverses. Oberon also has magical powers and knows the properties of herbs and charms to go with them. He can make himself invisible and he and his queen can fly through the air at astonishing speed: "We the globe can compass soon/ Swifter than the wandering moon." Finally, Oberon has the ability to dispense health and good fortune on couples and their offspring, blessing them with nothing more than enchanted field dew.[6]

OBERON'S LATER CAREER

Fairy kings and queens had been known in British folklore during the sixteenth century, but with the exception of Mab, they had not been named. In taking his character from *Huon of Bordeaux*, Shakespeare accelerated Oberon to the forefront of the fairy court.

Oberon was seen next in Dekker's *Whore of Babylon* (1607), in which he featured once again as Henry VIII, father to Elizabeth I, who appeared in the guise of Titania. This role evidently owes a great deal more to Spenser than it does to Shakespeare's relatively recently performed play. Thereafter,

---

5 Act III, 2.
6 Act IV, 1; Act V, 2.

Oberon's position as head of the faery court was secure. For example, two fraudsters, John and Alice West, tried to cheat a London widow of her money and goods in about 1612 and, as part of this ploy, they told the woman that Oberon had become enraged when he heard that she had spoken to others about his intended bounty towards her. The Wests' threat to cover up their deceit coupled the well-known hatred of the fairies for a person who blabbed about their generosity with reference to what, by then, must have been the acknowledged name of the fairy monarch.[7]

In June 1610 Ben Jonson staged a masque, *Oberon the Fairy Prince,* in which the eponymous young prince was surrounded by elves, faes, nymphs and satyrs. The fact that Oberon is the husband of Queen Mab in Drayton's *Nymphidia* (1627) would seem to reflect further his newly confirmed primacy as the pre-eminent fairy king. The role needed no longer to be fulfilled anonymously. However, Oberon does not appear favourably in this miniature epic – perhaps another inheritance from *Midsummer Night's Dream*. He is a proud monarch who is at risk of being cuckolded and who is consumed by a jealous rage. He enjoys 'making sport' in human homes at night, yet at the same time he is filled with suspicion and jealously over one of his knights, Pigwiggen, whom he suspects of dallying with the queen. As a result, Oberon grows "as mad as any Hare," becoming so "Bedlam" (mad and frantic) that he strikes out at any innocent male he comes across and plots vengeance upon his wife and her lover. The king's anger culminates in a joust with Pigwiggen. Fortunately for all concerned, Proserpina intervenes before serious injuries are inflicted; she uses her magic to make all the parties forget their quarrel and to restore peace and harmony in Faery.

Oberon was also undisputed prince of the faeries in Thomas Randolph's *Amyntas, or the Impossible Dowry,* written in 1632. The youthful king's realm is described as a utopia and he has "a stately presence," seated upon his "throne of state." He leads an

---

7 *The Cousenages of the Wests*, London, 1613.

enviably "delitious life" surrounded by milkmaids and nymphs with kisses "as sweet as sillibubs." Yet, he is also called "Prince of Pigmies" and is portrayed being caught stealing apples from an orchard.[8] For all his regal qualities, then, Oberon is prey to the baser human emotions and his conduct can degenerate into farce. He need not be taken fully seriously.[9]

Once Oberon had been established as the unquestioned king of fairyland, authors could then proceed to make literary experiments with him, knowing that his regal status was secured. In William Browne's *Britannia's Pastorals* Oberon is featured enjoying a miniscule banquet,[10] a conceit that was subsequently taken up and expanded upon by Robert Herrick in a series of poems concerning "mighty Oberon," his queen, their palace, its chapel and a feast they enjoy. Herrick leaves us in no doubt as to the splendour of the faery court (however microscopic it may be), with its elaborate buildings and its lavish entertainments. Oberon sits down to a banquet of many delicate courses washed down with dew and honey wine. What's more:

"… all this while his eye is serv'd,
We must not think his eare was sterv'd."

A consort of grasshopper, cricket, fly and gnat provide music as the king feasts. At the end of this elegant repast Oberon is "high fed/ For Lust and action" whilst the wine has worked to "bewitch/ His blood to height." Accordingly, he is led by his courtiers to other pleasures:

"Halfe tipsie to the Fairie Bed,
Where Mab he finds; who there doth lie
Not without mickle majesty."

In the queen's splendid and sumptuous bed chamber, Oberon is undressed by his attendants, who then discretely depart:

---

8 From *Amyntas*, respectively Act I, scene 3; I, 6; IV, 6 and III, 4.
9 See too Randolph's *Jealous Lovers*, c.1632.
10 Browne, 1624–8, Book III, song 1.

"And now the bed and Mab possest,
Of this great-little-kingly-Guest.
We'll nobly think, what's to be done,
He'll do no doubt..."[11]

Very similar to these more famous verses is a short poem attributed to Sir Simeon Steward, *The Fairy King, or Oberon Dressing,* which was published posthumously in 1635. It depicts the monarch being dressed by his servants in clothes made from cobwebs, flies' wings and grasses. The humour in these poems is whimsical, but we must admit that Oberon's majesty is left as diminished as his stature by the work of Herrick, Steward and Drayton.[12]

Since the seventeenth century, Oberon's dominion on the fairy throne has remained unchallenged. He has been kept in the public eye through a variety of media. The publication in Germany in 1780 of Christoph Martin Wieland's epic *Oberon* marked the beginning of a reinvigorated interest in his story. The poem was based on *Huon of Bordeaux* and soon generated its own adaptations and imitations. Actress Friedericke Sophie Seyler used the verses to create a *Singspiel* titled *Huon und Amande,* which in turn was copied in 1789 to form the libretto for the opera, *Oberon, König der Elfen,* by Austrian composer Paul Wranitzky. Carl Maria von Weber also used the poem, as translated by J.R. Planche, for the basis for his last opera, *Oberon – or the Elf King's Oath,* in 1826. Interestingly, its first performance at the Theatre Royal, Covent Garden, in London, in April of that year, was advertised with playbills that promoted its spectacular scenery. These included 'Oberon's Bower,' a 'Ravine amongst the Rocks of a Desolate Island' and a 'Perforated Cavern on the Beach,' which was seen successively with the ocean lashed by a storm, in a calm and at sunset. These sorts of elaborate production became part and parcel of faery theatre and pantomime as the subsequent decades passed.

---

11 Herrick, *Oberon's Feast* and *Oberon's Palace.*
12 See too Mary Elizabeth Robinson (1775–1818), *Oberon to Titania,* in which he invites his "tiny love" to sip dew from an acorn goblet; John Keats, *On Receiving a Curious Shell*; Kate Seymour Maclean, *Pansies.*

Other operatic versions of the story include William Sotheby's *Oberon, or a Mask in Five Parts* (1803), the anonymous *The Gnome King: An Elfin Freak, or Legend of Number-Nip* (1819) and George Macfarren's *Oberon, or the Charmed Horn* (1826). Wieland's work was also adapted into a ballet, *Sire Huon*, by Michael Costa in 1834. Inspiration travelled in the opposite direction as well. Felix Mendelssohn composed music for a version of *The Dream* based upon a translation into German by August Wilhelm Schlegel and Ludwig Tieck.

King Oberon was influential in the fine arts as well. Fuseli illustrated an edition of Wieland's poem in 1795. His king in the scene *Oberon Drips Flower Sap in Sleeping Titania's Eyes* (1793–4) is a muscular monarch akin to a Greek sculpture, dressed in a short cloak with a sceptre and standing imperiously over his semi-naked queen. Puck appears in the background, looking like a masked Greek player. In 1888 Sir Noel Paton portrayed *Oberon Watching a Mermaid* in a very similar way. The fairy king is a slim, athletic youth, crowned with butterfly wings. He gazes longingly at the naked mermaid, reclining like a John Simmons fairy on a rock offshore, whilst an imp-like Puck crouches nearby, grinning mischievously to himself. He is a boy, but with large pointed ears and furled bat wings that are leathery and black. David Scott version of this scene, which Paton must have known, but his Oberon looks more like a Greek shepherd with a robe around his waist, whilst Puck is a curious butterfly winged character.

Oberon reigned in poet Thomas Tickell's epic *Kensington Gardens* (1722) and, along with Queen Mab, in Thomas Parnell's verse *A Fairy Tale in the Ancient English Style*, published in the same year, as well as in numerous subsequent poems. We meet the king, for instance, Thomas Hood's *Plea of the Midsummer Fairies* (in which he carries a wand) and in John Keats' *The Song of the Four Fairies*.[13] He is a woodland monarch still in Alfred Noyes' *Song of Sherwood*, demonstrating how the link with the natural

---

13 See too Bulwer-Lytton, *To the Ideal*; Victor James Daley, *A Christmas Eve*; William Wordsworth, *The Triad*; Madison Cawein, *Willow Wood*.

environment, established in *Huon of Bordeaux* and reinforced by Shakespeare, has been maintained into modern times.[14]

For Edna St Vincent Millay, in *Doubt No More* of 1921, Oberon seems to have become part and parcel of the English landscape, as he leads a fairy band "Over the indulgent land."[15] Horace Walpole writing a letter in January 1764, granted Oberon even greater dominion, gracing him with the titles of "grand [and] emperor of fairyland," so that we should not be at all surprised to meet "imperial Oberon" in William Allingham's *Prince Brightkin,* published in 1877.[16]

Oberon's reputation as a healer, or wizard, skilled with herbs, also lingered about him. Frances Greville (1724–89) addressed her *Prayer for Indifference* to the (tiny) fairy king, bidding him to:

> "haste to shed the sovereign balm,
> My shatter'd nerves new string;
> And for my guest, serenely calm,
> The nymph Indifference bring!"

She sought from the monarch tranquil days and nights of calm repose, freed from worries over herself and others.[17]

Howsoever his dominion has expanded, Oberon has never fully regained his adult dimensions. He remains miniscule, as in the verse *A Fairy Family* by Sydney Dobell (1824–74). In this, the noble prince of a "tiny band" lives under a stone, eats grass seeds and drinks milk from the drops caught in flowers beneath a cow during milking. For his leisure, the king goes sailing on a beetle's wing. An undated poem, *The Fairies' Umbrella,* included in Frances Jenkins Olcott's *Book of Elves and Fairies* describes an equally miniature monarch and his court:

---

14 See too Walter de la Mare, *Widow's Weeds*; Sydney Dobell, *Grass from the Battlefield*; Madison Cawein, *The Berriers.*
15 But see Keat's *Lamia Part One,* for a more martial Oberon.
16 *Letters of Horace Walpole,* 1890, vol.1.
17 See too William Cowper, *To Miss Macartney* and Barron Field, *Botany Bay Flowers.*

"I spied King Oberon and his beauteous Queen
Attended by a nimble-footed train
Of Fairies tripping o'er the meadow's green,
And to mewards (methought) they came amain.
I couched myself behind a bush to spy,
What would betide the noble company.
It 'gan to rain, the King and Queen they run
Under a mushroom, fretted overhead,
With glow-worms artificially done,
Resembling much the canopy of a bed
Of cloth of silver: and such glimmering light
It gave, as stars do in a frosty night."[18]

All the standard fairy conceits (both traditional and literary) are here – dancing in green places, glow-worm lamps and mushrooms as proportionate shelters, as well as the named king.[19]

Oberon is today accepted as the archetypal fairy king and, it's true, he clearly has some Old English roots, but he's come to us by way of literature and is not really a true folklore figure. For the British, though, this need not really matter because they've had their own native fairy king all along, whose name is Arthur – as we shall discover in a later chapter.

18 Olcott, *The Book of Elves & Fairies*, New York, 1918, 212.
19 See too William Allingham, *The Daffodil*; or Robert Henry Forster, *Sweet Peas*.

CHAPTER SEVEN

King Arthur

Readers might be surprised to find Arthur included in a list of faery characters. He is, it might be supposed, more properly a king of legend rather than of fairy tale. However, such is Arthur's fame that he has transcended boundaries. King Arthur long ago ceased to be merely a Dark Age hero or monarch of the Round Table: he was transformed into a supernatural being and a resident of Faery.

FOUNDATIONS OF THE MYTH

According to the several versions of the story, after Arthur was mortally wounded fighting his nephew Mordred, he was carried away to Avalon to be healed by the fay maidens Morgan and Nimue. From this myth of fairy salvation, a closer link to fairy nature evolved – and this at a very early date, well before the legends became internationally famous.

The starting point for these developments in the story of Arthur seems to have been the very early awareness that his place of burial was unknown. An old Welsh poem called *Y Beddau* (The Graves) recites where many kings and heroes were buried, but it concludes, enigmatically, *"Anoeth bid bet y Arthur"* – "The grave of Arthur is a mystery."[1] If the great national hero had no known resting place, the scope for speculation about his fate was obvious and we know for certain that it took place. For example, some canons from Laon in France made a fundraising visit to England in 1113. They toured the country and, at Bodmin in Cornwall, got into a violent dispute with a local over the lost king. The author of the record of this incident, Hermann

---

1 M. Pennar, *The Black Book of Carmarthen*, 1989, 104.

of Tournai, observed "Just as the Bretons are wont to wrangle with the French on behalf of King Arthur," so the man in Bodmin insisted vehemently that Arthur was still alive.[2]

Arthur had achieved some sort of immortality, reports of which were in very active circulation during the twelfth century. William of Malmesbury wrote a history of the kingdom of England in 1125, noting that "The tomb of Arthur is nowhere to be seen, whence ancient ditties fable that he is yet to come." In 1155, another historian, Wace, recorded the widespread belief that Arthur:

> "is yet in Avalon, awaited by the Britons; for, as they say and deem, he will return from whence he went and live again. Master Wace cannot add more to what was said by Merlin. He said that Arthur's end should be hidden in doubtfulness. Merlin spoke truly. Men have ever doubted and, as I am persuaded, ever will doubt whether he is alive or dead."

Of course, some would argue that this 'fable' should have been dismissed once and for all as fantasy in 1190, when the alleged tomb of Arthur and Guinevere was 'discovered' at Glastonbury Abbey. This was, though, plainly a fake: the bodies were marked by a lead cross stating that the king and queen had been buried "in the Isle of Avalon," as if anyone attending the burial or visiting the sepulchre subsequently might not have known where they were... [3]

Discovered tombs notwithstanding, Arthur was immortal and he was not to be suppressed. In his history of England called the *Brut*, which dates to around 1190, the monk Layamon added an important new layer to this persistent story:

> "*Bruttes ileveð ȝete þat he beon on live,*
> *And wunnien in Avalun mid fairest alre alfen...*"

---

2 E.K. Chambers, *Arthur of Britain*, 1927, 18.

3 Chambers, *Arthur of Britain*, 17, citing *De Rebus Gestis Regum Anglorum*, Book III, 287; Wace, *Roman de Brut*.

"The British believe yet that he is alive,
And dwells in Avalon with the fairest of all the elves."

In the thirteenth century French romance of *Huon of Bordeaux*,
Arthur even succeeds King Oberon to the fairy throne. Historian
Raphael Holinshed, in 1578, told much the same story. He
reported that Britons still "fantasticallie doo descant and report
wonders" about Arthur. He mocked the entire myth, whether
there had ever been such a king as well as the notion that he
might return to rule again. Nevertheless, he revealed that
Layamon's vision of the hero's fate was still current: "King
Arthur was not dead, but carried away by the fairies into some
pleasant place..."[4]

Poet John Lydgate in the fifteenth century had developed this
aspect of the story even further, though, and had the fairy king
return to rule us:

"He is a king y-crowned in Faërie,
With his sceptre and pall, and with his regalty,
Shalle resort, as lord and sovereigne,
Out of Faërie and reign in Bretaine,
And repair again the oulde Rounde table."[5]

The *Morte d'Arthur,* published by Thomas Malory in 1485, is
one of the most influential versions of the legend. The author
preferred not to commit himself upon the king's fate: "Thus of
King Arthur I find no more written in my copy of the certainty of
his death;" after he sailed away with Morgan and Nimue, "More
of the death of King Arthur, I could never find." A body had been
buried, he said, "but yet the hermit knew not of a certain that it
was verily the body of King Arthur." Lastly –

"Some men say in many parts of England that King Arthur
is not dead, but had by the will of our lord Jesus Christ

---

4 *Chronicles*, Book V, c.14.
5 *The Fall of Princes*, 1431–8, Book VIII, c.24

gone into another place, and men say that he will come again and he shall win the holy cross. I will not say it shall be so, but rather I will say – here in this world he changed his life. But many men say that written on his tomb is this verse: *Hic jacet Arthurus, rex quondam, rexque futurus* [Here lies Arthur, the once and future king]."[6]

This was, of course, all very odd as a conclusion to a book called 'The Death of Arthur.' Malory was not prepared to dismiss completely the very longstanding belief in the king's altered state and his potential return. This may have been because he wished to believe the stories, because he did not wish to upset those of his readers who treasured that myth or, perhaps, because it simply provided a good 'cliff hanger' ending to his epic. Whatever Malory's reasons, the mystery of Arthur's death or transformation were perpetuated for future generations.

By being taken to Faery, Arthur (perhaps by consuming the food and drink there) had become immortal himself and now awaits the call to return to save his former kingdom. So, our saviour Arthur was believed to sleep on with the fairies in many places around Britain: under Arthur's Seat, Edinburgh, in Wales at Craig-y-Ddinas, Ogo'r Dinas, and Pumsaint near Lampeter, and, in England, at Sewingshields, Richmond and Cadbury, to name but a few of the locations.

In fact, fairy glamour quickly enveloped the king completely. According to the romance *Brut de la Montaigne*, all fairy haunted places belong to Arthur,[7] whilst in Gerbert's *Romance of Percival*, the 'siege perilous' at the Round Table was bestowed upon Arthur by "*la fée de la roche menor*" (the fairy of the menhir). Many of the knights of his court too, such as Gawain and Lancelot, have fairy origins: Lancelot, for example, is raised by the mere-maid, the Lady of the Lake. Chaucer, in the *Squire's Tale*, described for his audiences –

6 Malory, *Morte D'Arthur*, Book III, chapters 167 & 168.
7 Verses XXX & XXXI.

"That Gawain with olde curtesie
Though he were come agen out of faerie."

What's more, the time of Arthur's rule began to be seen as one especially favourable to the fairy presence in Britain, during which, far and wide, they danced openly in pastures and meadows. Thus, in his version of Chaucer's *The Wife of Bath – Her Tale*, John Dryden invoked memories of how:

"In days of old, when Arthur fill'd the throne,
Whose acts and fame to foreign lands were blown,
The king of elves and tiny fairy queen
Gambolled on heaths and danced on every green."

Thomas Parnell (1679–1718), in *A Fairy Tale in the Ancient English Style,* similarly sought to revive a golden age "In Britain's isle, and Arthur's days,/ When midnight fairies danced the maze."

ARTHUR, VICTORIA AND MERRY ENGLAND

"They told me in their shadowy phrase,
Caught from a tale gone by,
That Arthur, King of Cornish praise,
Died not, and would not die.

Dreams they had, that in fairy bowers
Their living warrior lies,
Or wears a garland of the flowers
That grow in Paradise."[8]

During the nineteenth century, Arthur came to lie at the heart of English culture. The fascination of poets and painters with the many aspects and personalities of his story can be seen as

---

8 Robert Hawker, *To Alfred Tennyson.*

part of a wider revival of interest in Gothic and Old English materials. To name but a handful, the poets Alfred Tennyson and William Morris and the Pre-Raphaelite movement found profound inspiration in the romances, most especially in the pages of Malory. In his *Idylls of the King*, Lord Tennyson renewed our hopes of a supernatural national saviour, confirming how the Fairy Queen would–

> "… come to take the King to Fairyland,
> For some do hold our Arthur cannot die,
> But that he passes into Fairyland."[9]

Later English poet Philip James Bailey (1816–1902) took the medieval associations with Arthur even further in his epic verse *A Spiritual Legend*. He conjured up "fairy Avalon, still where Arthur rules,/ Sole as the sun in heaven his shining shrine;" his island of Britain, meanwhile, was a mystical landscape of moors:

> "With cromlech crowned, gray cairn, or fairy knoll;
> Or lithic dance of giants 'neath the moon;"

These ancient sites, what's more, are scented with wild flowers:

> "all good spirits love perfumes
> With many an odorous plant, both hill and vale;
> Angelica, and honeyed melilot;
> Day's-eye and king-cup; fairy foxglove, fern;
> And violet…"

Arthur here is woven into a dense mythology of megalithic mystery, the British landscape and its supernatural denizens, becoming a spirit of place, a *genius loci*, as well as a hero and fairy monarch.

The conjunction of fairy stories and Arthurian myths still remains compelling to us now, precisely because it combines

---

9 Tennyson, *Lancelot and Elaine*, 1859, lines 1249–51.

magic and mystery along with a promise of redemption and restoration. The once and future king will return from Faery to assist us in our greatest struggle and to ensure our salvation. The exact nature of our 'hour of need' is undefined, but this leaves it mutable, ever adaptable and perpetually to be fulfilled. Arthur's restoration is our abiding hope and in a contemporary eschatology has attached itself to the ecological crisis.

CHAPTER EIGHT

Other Faery Kings & Heroes

We are all very familiar with the concept of faery queens, whether from Mab, Titania or from Spencer's famous poem, and British folk tradition gives the strong impression that they are widespread. Other than Oberon, faery kings are rather less frequently mentioned. We hear of an unnamed monarch in the poem *King Orfeo*, the 'eldritch king' of the ballad *Sir Cawline*, the elf king of *Leesom Brand* and, finally, the small faery man of the ballad the *Wee Wee Man* seems to be some sort of faery ruler or noble.[1]

As mentioned earlier, the sixteenth century Scottish poet Montgomerie wrote of "the King of Pharie with the court of the Elph-quene.' It's not apparent whether there is any major significance to his choice of wording, which seems at least to imply that the king is in some manner subservient to his consort. Interrogated in 1647 over allegations of sorcery, Margaret Alexander of Livingston claimed sexual relations with the faery king; she told the court that her affair with him had gone on for thirty years. Isobel Gowdie claimed that she had visited the fairy monarchs in their halls and described the king as a "braw man, weill favoured."[2]

The Herefordshire story of *King Herla* has an extended account of a faery king, although we never discover his name. Rather like the Oberon of *Huon of Bordeaux*, his appearance is rather un-regal: he looked like Pan, with "a large head, glowing

---

1 See my *Fairy Ballads & Rhymes*.
2 Montgomerie, *Flyting Between Montgomerie & Polwart*, 1515; A. Macdonald, 'A Witchcraft Case of 1647,' *Scots Law Times*, April 10th, 1937, 77; Pitcairn, *Ancient Criminal Trials in Scotland*, vol.3, Part 2, 602.

face and a long red beard... The lower part of his body was rough and hairy and his legs ended in goats' hooves." He was a dwarf – "a pygmy no bigger than an ape, and of less than human stature" – hence he was able to ride on a goat. Looks notwithstanding, he told Herla he was "lord over many kings and princes, over a vast and innumerable people." Certainly, his clothes – and those of his courtiers – were magnificent and he treated the guests at his wedding lavishly.

In summary, just as with the many faery queens encountered in folklore accounts, there were understood to be multiple faery kings, each monarch of their own small kingdom. [3]

RHYS DWFN

We know of two named kings of the Welsh faeries, the *tylwyth teg*. The first is the mysterious Rhys Dwfn, a monarch known by reputation but who is never actually encountered in stories.

Off the coast of south and west Wales there are some elusive islands inhabited by the *tylwyth teg*, or more specifically by the *Plant Rhys Dwfn* – the children of Rhys the Deep. The islands appear and disappear and are extremely difficult for mortals to reach from the mainland of Dyfed. Their king, Rhys, was described as 'deep' or wise in the sense that he protected his land and people from human intrusions using magic herbs. In addition, he instituted a strict moral code of honesty and good faith that continued to be observed by his descendants. They had no traitors in their community and they cared for all generations equally. These qualities, they remarked, set them apart from humankind and – it has to be said – from many other faery folk as well.[4]

Rhys' subjects were said to have been handsome but very small; they would invisibly visit human markets on the mainland and buy their provisions there, their mere presence apparently causing prices to rise. They are reported to have favoured, in succession, the markets at Cardigan, Fishguard and Haverfordwest.

3 E. Leather, *Folklore of Herefordshire*, 1912.
4 Rhys *Celtic Folklore* 158–160.

GWYNN AP NUDD

Older still than Rhys as king of the Welsh faeries is Gwynn ap Nudd. He is known as the monarch of the Welsh underworld (*Annwn*) in the myths of the *Mabinogion*; later he was seen the leader of his own tribe or nation of faeries, the *Plant Annwn* (the family or clan of Annwn) or, in Christian interpretations, ruler of hell and overlord of all the demons. Amongst his supernatural subjects are numbered the Welsh lake maidens, the *gwragedd annwn*, and the 'hell hounds' called the *cwn annwn*, which Gwynn is said to lead in a 'wild hunt' of lost souls, riding a black horse.[5]

Gwynn is also known because he invited the Welsh saint Collen to feast with him in his castle on top of Glastonbury Tor. The saint was living at the foot of the hill as a hermit and, having rebuked some locals for expressing a belief in Gwynn, was invited to a feast in his hall. Collen attended reluctantly, and was confronted with a sumptuous banquet and a rich court. The holy man saw through the faeries' glamour, though; he could tell that he was being offered only leaves to eat rather than lavish dishes and, in contempt, he threw holy water over the assembly, making it scatter and vanish.

It seems that, over and above his basic powers of glamour, Gwynn had extra magical knowledge – as would befit a king. The *Welsh Triads* state that he had great knowledge about the stars and their influences: "Such was [his] knowledge of the stars, their natures and qualities, that [he] could prognosticate whatever was wished to be known until the day of doom. and could predict the future from them." It is, perhaps, for this reason that the Cornish story of *The House on Silena Moor* mentions the pixies worshipping stars, what might be a relic of much older British folk knowledge.[6]

---

5   See Evans Wentz, *Fairy Faith*, 319–320; Rhys, *Celtic Folklore*, vol.2, 438.
6   Iolo Morganwg, *Triads of Britain*, 1807, no.89.

EVELING

Even less well known is the mysterious King Eveling of Ravenglass in Cumbria. He was said to hold court at Lyon's Yards, the ruined Roman bath-house that stands near to the small seaside town, but other than that very little is known of him. This faery king is an intriguing figure because of his mythological connections: his name may very well be connected to Avalloc, putative ruler of the island of Avalon; both have some connection to Evelake, King of Sarras, who is found in the later French romances of Arthur. Eveling was, then, a significant figure at one time, but almost all details of him have been lost, in addition to which both he and Gwyn have been eclipsed first by Arthur and then by Oberon.

TOM THUMB

In the seventeenth century Tom Thumb was a small elf well-known to people through ballads and rhymes. He is mentioned as a typical faery figure by Reginald Scot, in his list of famous characters, and was recorded later by Denham. Since then, he has been caught up by romance and fairy-tale and has lost almost all of his supernatural nature.

Drayton, in *Nimphidia* (1627), mentioned Tom as a "fairy page" whilst in the *Ballad of Robin Goodfellow* he played a bagpipe for faery dancing. Later still in the seventeenth century, poet Margaret Cavendish also identified Tom as the page to the faery queen.[7]

However, other authors of the period had a loftier vision of Tom. According to a pamphlet written by Richard Johnson in 1621, and turned into verse in 1630, Tom was a knight in the court of King Arthur.[8] He was only an inch high, or a quarter of a span, but he was still a valiant man. His father was a

---

7 Cavendish, *The Pastime of the Queen of Fairies, when she comes upon the Earth out of the Centre.*

8 J. Halliwell, *The Nursery Rhymes of England*, 1886, LXI.

humble ploughman, but his birth was magical: with Merlin's aid the boy was conceived and born within half an hour. Tom is not entirely human, clearly, which is underlined by the fact that, as Merlin warns, "He shall have life, but substance not; No blood, nor bones in him shall grow." This lack of skeleton may possibly connect him to the nursery sprite Boneless and so imply a clear faery origin. Certainly, his is birth was attended by the fairy queen, who provided him with suitably faery clothing, such as an oak leaf hat and a shirt of spider's web. Tom later has notable abilities, such as being able to creep through keyholes, a standard form of faery entry to human homes.

After various mishaps and adventures, Tom joined Arthur's court as the king's dwarf and performed many chivalrous deeds. Eventually, he sickened and died, whereupon his spirit was taken into fairyland by the queen and her "dancing nymphs in green." Tom's status therefore appears to be that of faery favourite rather than being a faery as such. He is favoured by a faery godmother, who is certain versions gives him a variety of protective powers, whilst at the end of his life he is carried off to Faery, very much like King Arthur himself, the enchanted realm seeming something akin to heaven.

The list in Part Two of the *Denham Tracts* (see the Foreword) includes 'Tom Thumbs' and, in addition, 'Tom Tumblers.' This character is known as an identifiable individual from a couple of seventeenth century sources.

In Vipian Fulwell's 1587 play, *A Pleasant Enterlude, intituled, Like Will to Like Quoth the Devill to the Collier*, when the devil first enters, a character exclaims "Sancte Benedicite, who have we heere? Tom tumbler or els some dauncing beare." In John Fletcher's play *The Island Princess, or, The Generous Portugal*, which was first published in 1669, there is a similar reference – "you wou'd a thought Tom Tumbler and all his Troop… had been there." These texts seem to indicate pretty strongly (as indeed does the name itself) that Tom Tumbler is a generic name for an acrobatic entertainer, a performer of somersaults. This would suggest that the name only ended up in the Denham list because of a passing resemblance to Tom Thumb.

There must be more to Tom Tumbler than that though. He is likened to the devil – as well as to a dancing bear. As well shall see in a later chapter, Robin Goodfellow/ Puck often took this form or was compared to it because of his hairiness. There appears to be some supernatural or demonic connotation here, then. In addition, a correspondent to *Notes and Queries* in 1867 suggested that Tom Tumbler might be another colloquial name for the will of the wisp.[9]

JACK HORNER

The life of Robin Goodfellow laid out in the seventeenth century chapbooks is closely mirrored by that of Jack Horner, as is recorded in *The pleasant History of Jack Horner, containing his witty Tricks and pleasant Pranks, which he plaied from his Youth to his riper Years* – published in about 1790.

Jack is a diminutive figure, barely one foot in height (but still "a giant to Tom Thumb") and is best known from the traditional nursery rhyme associated with him:

> "Little Jack Horner sat in the corner,
> Eating a Christmas pie;
> He put in his thumb, and he took out a plum,
> And said, "What a good boy am I!"[10]

When Jack grows up, he proceeds to have a series of adventures in which (just like Robin) he helps the poor and saves the weak and defenceless. Ultimately, he kills a giant and marries his daughter, thereby becoming a squire. Jack is brave and bold, but he has no magical powers and no faery ancestry – rather his father seems to be an ordinary mortal. Accordingly, whilst his story is modelled upon that of Robin Goodfellow, Jack is not a supernatural.

---

9 *Notes and Queries*, Third Series, volume 11, January 5th 1867, 23–24.
10 J. Halliwell, *The Nursery Rhymes of England*, 1886, 65.

CHAPTER NINE

Ariel

A riel is *not* one of the traditional members of the British fairy clan. He is almost entirely an invention of Shakespeare for his play *The Tempest* and, in truth, it is not even clear whether or not the character is a fairy or some other sort of spirit. These uncertainties notwithstanding, the popularity of Shakespeare's characters have cemented Ariel in the public consciousness and he is most easily understood as being of the fairykind.

The character Ariel in Shakespeare's *The Tempest* is a distinct departure from the fairies of the playwright's earlier *Midsummer Night's Dream*. Both Ariel and Puck conjure illusions out of glamour on their masters' behalf, but in the latter play, Puck is derived straight from British folk tradition with his pranks, his earthy humour and his domestic associations. Ariel has none of these characteristics, yet he is still a "tricksy spirit." Where did Shakespeare get his inspiration? There are three separate Ariels whom we must discuss.[1]

ORIGINS

Ariel is a Hebrew name. Heinrich Cornelius Agrippa mentions in *De Occulta Philosophia* that "Ariel is the name of an angel, and is the same as the Lion of God. Sometimes it is also the name of an evil demon and of a city called Ariopolis where the idol of Ariel was worshipped."[2] The name was chosen by medieval and Renaissance magicians, and by Neo-Platonist philosophers, for one of the sylphs, a being who was sometimes said to be ruler of Africa. Sylphs are one of the four 'elementals', the spirits of the earth, air, fire and water. The sylphs are the spirits of the air

---

1 *Tempest* Act V scene 1.
2 Agrippa, Book III, Part 3.

and are reputed to be capricious, passionate and irascible. Their airy and aerial connections obviously suggested a fairy analogy to playwrights and poets and this Neo-Platonist being must be a likely inspiration for Shakespeare.

SHAKESPEARE'S SPIRIT

In *The Tempest* the spirit Ariel is enslaved by the sorcerer Prospero. He has many very typical fairy traits: he can become invisible; he can fly at incredible speed ("with a twink"), riding on the clouds and conjuring storms; he can walk on the waves and ride the sharp north wind; finally, and most importantly, he can change his shape.

As Floris de Lattre observed "Ariel himself is not without some likeness to Puck. He also is a preternatural courier and flies nimbly through the air on his master's missions. He is more refined, however ... than Oberon's body-servant, though once, at least, he fairly treats himself to a Puck-like trick when his invisible interference leads to blows between Trinculo and Stephano."[3]

Ariel is a winged spirit – 'delicate,' 'a bird', a 'chick,' he is 'but air.' His 'dainty' and diminutive nature is emphasised by the song he sings:

> "Where the bee sucks, there suck I:
> In a cowslip's bell I lie;
> There I couch when owls do cry.
> On the bat's back I do fly
> After summer merrily.
> Merrily, merrily shall I live now
> Under the blossom that hangs on the bough."[4]

Ariel was formerly imprisoned in a tree by a witch; from this Prospero released him – on conditions of service for a time.

---

3 *English Fairy Poetry*, 116–117.
4 Act V, scene 1

After a period serving Prospero well and faithfully, Ariel is ultimately released: "to the elements be free" and then is "as free as mountain winds."[5]

Ariel's relationship to wider faery kind is indicated by his diminutive size, hiding in flowers just like the fairies of *Midsummer Night's Dream*. In addition, there is his song 'Come unto these yellow sands,' which is addressed to 'sweet sprites' and which subsequent generations have certainly assumed to refer to dancing fairies: see for example the paintings by Robert Huskisson (1841) and Richard Dadd (1842) which take their title from the song. Furthermore, Ariel's association with music, song and dance in itself indicates a faery nature and his use of these to lead the plays other characters around the island is very much like 'pixie leading.'[6]

Later writers have certainly accepted Ariel's faery identity. In the poem *Ariel In The Cloven Pine* by James Bayard Taylor (1825–78), the spirit laments his imprisoned state and compares himself to "happier elves," whilst in her *Song of Ariel* (c.1811) Janetta Philips linked the sprite to fays, Titania and nymphs.[7]

Puck is clearly and solidly male, but Ariel is sexless (hence, in theatrical productions, the frequency with which the character is portrayed as either male or female). In contrast to Puck's cheeky cheeriness, Ariel seems subservient and melancholy. This theme of enslavement perhaps comes from Ariel's origins in hermetic magic: he is a familiar, a spirit to be conjured and commanded. He is there to do Prospero's will and lacks any personality or motivation of his own. Both captive Ariel and the conjured spirit are controlled by another's arcane knowledge and skills.

ALEXANDER POPE

There is a second Ariel in English literature. In Alexander Pope's *Rape of the Lock* (1714) Ariel the sylph reappears. The poem was

5 Act V scene 1 and Act II scene 1.
6 Act I, scene 2.
7 See too 'Ariel' by Albert Pike (1809–91).

a mock-heroic commentary upon an actual incident, first written in 1712, and the 'machinery' of the sylphs was something of an afterthought for Pope. Nevertheless, the elementals assume an important role as guardians and attendants to the heroine. In his introductory letter to Mrs Arabella Fermor that precedes the poem, Pope states that he has drawn upon "a very new and odd Foundation, the Rosicrucian doctrine of spirits." He explains to her that, according to these gentlemen, the four elements are inhabited by spirits, the sylphs being "the best condition'd Creatures imaginable. For they say, any mortals may enjoy the most intimate Familiarities with these gentle spirits, upon a Condition very easy to all true Adepts, an inviolate preservation of Chastity."

Chastity is key to Pope's plot. In the poem, Ariel's task is to protect his mistress Belinda's virtue, but as a sylph he seems ill-suited to do this. We also learn from the poem that women can be reborn as one or other of the elementals, depending upon their characteristics during life and that:

> "The light Coquettes in Sylphs aloft repair,
> And sport and flutter in the Fields of Air."[8]

Thanks to Pope's intervention, the sylphs began to transform into the explicitly tiny fairies with insect wings that are now so familiar to us. They have 'transparent forms' and 'fluid Bodies half dissolv'd in Light.'[9]

In the event, the Ariel of Pope's poem fails to protect Belinda's virginity and a symbolic lock of her hair is snipped off by a suitor. This contrasts with the success of Ariel in *The Tempest*, who fulfils all of Prospero's commands and so earns his release. It is significant that, having failed in his duty, Pope's Ariel is replaced by Umbriel, a malignant gnome (a daemon of the earth who delights in mischief, according to the Rosicrucian doctrine).

---

8 Canto I, lines 65–66.
9 Canto II lines 59–67.

VICTORIAN ARIEL AND AFTER

Just as *Midsummer Night's Dream* saw a revival in the Victorian theatre, so too did *The Tempest*. The play continued to be performed throughout the late seventeenth and eighteenth century, but in a heavily cut form. A production by William Charles Macready in 1838 restored the original text and a further renowned staging by Charles Kean in 1857 confirmed the popularity of the play thereafter. Interestingly, the convention in Victorian times (as in the previous century) was for a woman to play Ariel (although this was true for both Puck and Oberon as well, decisions which may seem far more surprising to us). Both Daniel Maclise and Richard James Lane R.A. painted actress Priscilla Horton as she appeared in the role in at the Theatre Royal in 1838. She is unquestionably a slender young woman in a dress, with her long hair decorated with foliage and a pair of gauzy fly wings.

The familiarity of the play to audiences inspired artists to begin to design works based upon scenes and characters from the text. The *Rape of the Lock*, meanwhile, had a rather more consistent history of illustration and from the start depictions of the sylphs were instrumental in shaping public perceptions of fairies.

The earliest artist to tackle Ariel as a subject was Henry Fuseli, who in *Belinda's Awakening* (1780–90) made the Pope's sylph a very solid and Puck-like being. He has a very robust and masculine physique and an unpleasant expression, the only gesture to effeminacy being a chaplet of flowers on his head. The same cannot be said of the work of Joseph Severn, who painted Shakespeare's Ariel twice. In the larger of the two scenes, from 1826, he is shown as a naked and very girlish boy riding a bat with a peacock feather in each hand. Severn may have drawn some inspiration from *Ariel on a Bat's Back*, exhibited by Henry Singleton at the Royal Academy in 1819, although the latter's sprite is a rather older and more athletic young man.

John Everett Millais created what is probably the most memorable painting of Ariel, showing him luring Ferdinand

(1849). Ariel looks like a green haired girl with web-like green wings; s/he floats along backwards before the young man, supported by eight green goblin bats. It is one of the oddest of all Victorian fairy paintings, although John Anster Fitzgerald's *Ariel* (1858–68) is also strange. Ariel is depicted there as a sexless being with a mass of golden curls who lies on a hawthorn branch, scattering may blossom towards the observer. He has dragonfly wings and a robe that dissolves into a mass of blossom. David Scott's much earlier *Ariel and Caliban*, from 1837, is closely comparable. The spirit floats above the deformed monster reclining on his back, long wings extended and golden hair streaming in the wind. An androgynous boy very similar to Fitzgerald's is seen again in Maud Tindal Atkinson's *Ariel* of 1915. Here the spirit, with crumpled turquoise butterfly wings, seems to hatch from the trunk of a pine tree. It is, once again, a unique vision.

A 1908 edition of the *Tempest* was illustrated by Edmund Dulac. His Ariel was another androgynous young male and he was equipped with feathered wings, making him more of an angel than a fairy. In one plate, however, he is transformed into a fearsome harpie, with eagle-like legs and claws and his arms merging into pinions. Arthur Bentley Connor painted *Prospero Releasing Ariel from the Tree* for the Shakespeare Memorial Theatre, Stratford, in 1911. His sprite is another smooth figured boy, with vaguely green wings resembling those of a fly; Louis Rhead's *Ariel* is another youth in a short robe, equipped with butterfly wings but riding pensively upon a bat. In 1931 Eleanor Fortescue-Brickdale illustrated another edition of *The Tempest*. Her *Prospero and Ariel* shows the spirit finally being set free by the magician; a very thin and insubstantial Ariel in a gauzy robe seems to spring into the air, arms thrown wide at his liberation. He has dragonfly wings, as do the other pale beings around him, one of whom holds her hands to the side of her head in a gesture very reminiscent of one of the green goblins in Millais' painting.

To conclude, Arthur Rackham's 1909 vision of Ariel also stayed true to this broad trend. He depicted a delicate fairy, an androgynous naked, long-haired male, sometimes portrayed with huge butterfly wings as seen in the illustration to the text 'When Caliban was lazy and neglected his work, Ariel would come slily and pinch him,' in which Ariel hovers over a monstrous Caliban. As was his style, Rackham drew the rest of the sprites and nymphs of the island as nude pubescent females.[10]

10 Illustrations to *Tales from Shakespeare*, Charles and Mary Lamb, 1909.

CHAPTER TEN

Puck and Robin Goodfellow

Puck is, very possibly, one of the most famous fairies in the world. This is entirely down to *Midsummer Night's Dream*, the effect of which has been to promote a humble hobgoblin to superstar status. At the time that the play was performed, though, it was Robin Goodfellow who was known and loved by all – this may very well explain the affectionate diminutive version of his name, Robinet, that is incorporated in Denham's faery list. Ultimately, the two characters, Puck and Robin, are one, but Shakespeare's success created an apparent duality which must be examined in this chapter.

PUCK IN ENGLISH FOLKLORE

Puck is now a fairy known to all nations, but until he was taken up by Shakespeare for *Midsummer Night's Dream,* there was no 'Puck,' but only 'pucks,' and these were just one type of hobgoblin amongst several. This much is apparent even in the *Dream*, in which reference is made to "an honest Puck" and "the Puck."[1] In the West of England, and down into the South-West, this being was well-known, whether as poake, pook, bucca or pixie.[2] Both Reginald Scot and the *Denham Tracts* make reference to a 'puckle,' which is likely to be a diminutive form of the name; it was preserved in the country name, *puckle's needle,* for any plants with pointed fruit (such as *Acus muscata*). English author Thomas Churchyard, who was born in Shrewsbury in

---

1 Burton, *Anatomy of Melancholy*, section 2; *Midsummer Night's Dream*, Act V, 1.
2 For full details of the latter, see my *British Pixies*, 2021.

1520, knew the species as "pretty little pogges." The puck's character was, by and large, mischievous but not malignant. He enjoyed a sort of rough humour and took considerable pleasure in discomforting humans.[3]

In Lancashire, Puck was even elevated to the position of "King o' the Fairies" in a story concerning the help that he gave to a farmer by labouring like a hob or brownie.[4] Overall, though, the sprite's reputation was poor. In *Epithalamion,* Edmund Spenser prayed for protection against supernatural assaults:

> "Ne let the Pouke, nor other evill sprights,
> Ne let mischivous witches with theyr charmes,
> Ne let hob Goblins, names whose sence we see not,
> Fray us with things that be not."

As can be seen, the puck was often equated with the devil. His name, certainly, is connected with terms like 'spook' (in German and Dutch) and with the Icelandic *puki,* an imp. If not outright malicious and demonic, Puck could be prone to playing practical tricks on people – most especially by leading them astray at night. We shall explore this habit in detail later, but here we may note that in Hampshire the sprite called the 'colt-pixy' would take equine form to lure horses into bogs and marshes, whilst in the North of England the pick-tree brag was another horse-like being who carried off hapless travellers and dumped them in pools. Elements in the names of both may seem to indicate a link to Puck.[5]

ROBIN'S FRIENDS & RELATIONS

Puck can be more fully understood if we examine some of those other British faeries, beings who are related to him. Across the British Isles there were forms of spirit whose name and/

3 Churchyard, *A Handful of Gladsome Verses,* 1592.
4 Bowker, *Goblin Tales of Lancashire,* 54.
5 See my *Faery Beasts,* 2020.

or habits linked them to the English puck. For instance, there were the Scots 'buckie' and 'pech,' the latter sometimes being confused with the historical people the Picts but, in fact, being a traditional Scottish pixie. Here, though, I shall focus on two other members of the family.

The Welsh Pwca

The original nature of the species or family called the pucks in England may perhaps be best divined by examining their Welsh cousin, the *pwca*. This being is also called *pwcca, bwcci, pwcci, brocci* and *pwica*.[6] Classed as one of the *ellyllon*, or elves, he is quite a local spirit, being concentrated in Breconshire and Monmouthshire. Within this limited area, though, he was evidently widespread: one local proverb stated that, at Halloween, you would find *"pwca ar bob camfa"* (a puck on every stile). It is reported that Shakespeare was familiar with Richard Price, prior of Brecon, and had visited his family home at nearby Scethrog, where he may have picked up stories about the *pwca*. This may be so, but it is unlikely to be the sole source for Puck.[7]

The *pwca's* character settles on two extremes. He can be described as both mischievous and malicious, much given to practical jokes, but he was also kindly and merry, being disposed to be helpful and to perform domestic and agricultural tasks for people.[8]

As a sort of domestic hob, the *pwca* might undertake tasks on farms such as cow-herding, in return for which he expected a conventional reward of milk and white (i.e. best quality) bread. On Aber Gwyddon farm, in Abercarn parish, Monmouthshire,

---

6 *North Wales Weekly News*, Jan. 15th 1909, 4; *The Cambrian*, Aug. 4th 1882, 3: some readers may recognise the latter name, as it is used in the TV series *Britannia* for the evil spirit who possesses the Druid Divis.

7 *Gwent Local History Journal*, Sept. 1st 1992, 15; *Cardiff & Merthyr Guardian*, March 26th 1853, 3.

8 *North Wales Weekly News*, Jan. 15th 1909, 4; *Wrexham & Denbighshire Advertiser*, April 20th 1878, 7; *South Wales Echo*, Feb. 9th 1894, 2.

the *pwca* is reported to have exercised violent revenge when the dairy maid left him only cold water and a crust one day. She was beaten and showered with insults for her meanness. As is so often the case with fairy kind, they will play tricks, but object bitterly when they themselves become the target of them. To avoid such revenge, it was reported as recently as 1891 that a farm maid at Llansannan (in Denbighshire in North Wales, it may be noted) would leave out milk for the *pwca* so that he would do her chores overnight; and they would be completed and the milk drunk by the morning.[9]

Another version of the *pwca's* history records that he was first known around Pontypool, but that he then removed to the area of Mynnyddislywn in Monmouth, travelling either in a jug of barm carried by a servant girl, or else in a ball of yarn. He then took up residence at Trwyn farm in the Gwyddon Valley, where he did chores such as hedging. For this, food was left out in the house for him, but if the customary reward was forgotten, he would make a mess, leaving dirt in the dairy. The *pwca* has also been located on Bryn Arw, to the east of Crickhowell and at Ty Pwca in Cwmbran.[10]

The *Pwca yr Trwyn* has been compared to a brownie, for he would also feed cattle and clean out their sheds in wet and wintry weather. His presence (rather like that of the *fynoderee* on the Isle of Man) was a guarantee of prosperity. This *pwca* was most commonly seen as a handful of grass, rolling along before the wind. This may be surprising, but it's not unique. The Dartmoor pixies have been described as looking like bundles of rags and certain boggarts can take on soft, rolling shapes as well.[11]

Despite his good qualities, the Trwyn *pwca* was laid or exorcised, being cast into the Red Sea for three generations. Writing in the mid-nineteenth century, it was reported by

---

9   John Rhys, *Celtic Folklore*, 1901, 147; *Carmarthen Journal*, Nov. 6th 1891, 8.

10 *The Nationalist*, vol.2, April 14th 1908; *Weekly Mail*, Jan. 25th 1902, 8 – 'Welsh Superstitions.'

11 *Notes & Queries*, vol.III, no.54, 1850, 388; *Cardiff & Merthyr Guardian*, Nov. 23rd 1850, 4; and see my *Beyond Faery*, 2020 & *Manx Faeries*, 2021.

folklorists that his imminent return was then anticipated by local people, meaning as it did that good times were coming.[12]

In Monmouthshire, the *pwca* was particularly associated with Cwm Pwca, also called Bucklands in English, which is just outside Clydach, near Blaenavon. The growth of the iron industry around here from the late eighteenth century was said to have largely driven the sprite away. The noise and smoke are likely to have repelled him; he preferred rural locations and soft pipe music.[13]

The other main manifestation of the Welsh *pwca* is as a congener of the English will of the wisp. In this form he is seen as a candle-like light that leads a benighted traveller off the road and towards a precipice. At the very last moment he will raise the light above his enormous head; then it will vanish and the *pwca* will leap over the cliff with a laugh, leaving his victim plunged in total darkness and having to struggle back to safety and the highway.[14]

A drawing of a *pwca* seen by a Welsh countryman, sitting on a milestone, shows him with a disproportionately large head and almost beak-like mouth.[15] As for leading travellers astray, it was as we know well established in England that this was one of the habits of the pucks, as Richard Burton described in the *Anatomy of Melancholy:* "As he (they say) that is led round about an heath with a Puck in the night."[16]

The Channel Islands Pouque

On the Channel Islands of Guernsey and Jersey, one of the main forms of faery is the *pouque,* a being especially associated with megalithic structures, the so-called *pouquelayes* – also spelled

---

12 *Pontypool Free Press*, Dec. 23rd 1876, 4.
13 *Bye Gones*, 1882, 274; *Welsh Outlook*, vol.11 no.2, Feb. 1st 1924, 'The Fiddler.'
14 *Cardiff Times*, Sept. 15th 1888, 1 – 'Welsh Gleanings.'
15 See Sikes, *British Goblins* or Crofton Croker, *Fairy Legends & Traditions*.
16 Burton, *Anatomy of Melancholy*, section II; See too Corbet's *Iter Borealis*.

pouclées, poucquelées and even *porquelées*.[17] This term is said to be a combination of two Breton or Celtic words, their form of 'puck' plus *lec'h* (a dolmen or cromlech – compare *llech*, a stone, in Welsh). An alternative translation of the second element is the Breton for 'place.' The pouques are said to have built the structures and may also continue to reside in them.[18]

The pouques – as on the British mainland – are often linked to the devil and are seen as separate from the communal faeries, the *faitots* or *p'tits gens*. They are described as being stunted and ugly, with a huge head, long powerful arms and unkempt hair. They can, apparently, live for several centuries. The pouques are also referred to as *le dain, le beu, le barboue, varou* (werewolf) and *le haptalaon* (snatch-heel).

The pouques are, on the whole, well-disposed towards humans, but they can be capricious and, sometimes, very bad tempered. On the positive side, they are prepared to help in farmers' fields, appearing in swarms to assist if a good deed is done for them. They might also look after children and guide travellers lost at night to safety. Conversely, they may attack people from time to time, for example because they have stayed up late gambling, and they may seek to abduct children, especially if those infants are stealing apples from orchards; then, their legs will be seized and they will be dragged off by the pouque. For all this apparent morality, the pouques are averse to Christian religion, which will drive them away.[19]

These pouques are not wholly anonymous. On Guernsey, Le P'tit Colin and Grand Colin (big and little Colin) are known; they are quite often associated with human homes and domestic tasks, but they have huge strength and are known for playing bat and ball with enormous stones. Colin is a name of French origin in English, ultimately deriving from Breton *cailean*, a young hound, which certainly seems to indicate its antiquity.

---

17 Philip Falle, *Caesaria*, 1734, 256.
18 *Monmouthshire Merlin*, Jan. 12th 1855, 2; J. Duncan, *History of Guernsey*, 1841, 372; see too chapter 11 of Young and Houlbrook, *Magical Folk*, 2018.
19 Marie de Garis, *Folklore of Guernsey*, 1975, 151 & 156.

ROBIN GOODFELLOW'S LIFE

Regionally familiar as pucks and pixies may have been, the hob that was universally known to English people during the sixteenth and seventeenth centuries was a being called Robin Goodfellow. He was a sort of hobgoblin or puck, but he had been distinguished from the anonymous mass of fairy with a personal name and epithet. The 'Goodfellow' label is just like the use of 'Good Neighbours' for the fairies, it is a mark of respect intended to appease a potentially powerful being – although with Robin it was also a mark of affection, as we shall see. Shakespeare was fully aware of the identity between these hobs and pucks – and that Robin was simply just a name for a puck. In the *Dream,* Puck is sometimes addressed as Robin, but the repeated usage of Puck as a term of address in the play had the perhaps unanticipated and unintentional effect of promoting this family name into a personal name, thereby displacing the traditional label.

A very strong sense of the importance of Robin Goodfellow ("otherwise called Hobgoblin") in early modern English culture may be gained from the fact that, in the early seventeenth century, two versions of his life were published, whilst several other texts traded upon his fame and his exploits.

The two 'biographies' were, firstly, the 1628 chap book *Robin Goodfellow, His Mad Pranks and Merry Jests,* a mainly prose text which incorporated a number of songs and rhymes, and which Katherine Briggs has labelled "a piece of popular journalism." Secondly, there was the *Ballad of Robin Goodfellow,* a version of the life story set out in the former book that had been edited down to its essentials in a handful of stanzas.[20] The main events of Robin's life described in both texts are as follows.

His mother was a young maid who was visited at night by a mysterious man. She discovered she was pregnant and, after the child was born, the absent father showered her and his son with

---

20 Briggs, *Dictionary of Fairies,* under 'Robin Goodfellow;' see too my *Fairy Ballads and Rhymes* (2020).

gifts to ensure that the boy was well-cared for. Many suspected that this man was a fairy, but the mother would only vouchsafe that "early in the morning he would go his way, whither she knew not, he went so suddainly."

The boy is christened Robin and proves to be a naughty child. When taken out by his mother, he constantly made faces at passers-by and was the source of constant complaints. His "jeering mocks and mowes" enraged his mother, who mourned that "these prankes no breeding shewes." She threatened her "vile untutored youth" with a beating if he did not reform – and Robin promptly ran away from her.

Robin soon found work as a tailor's apprentice and quickly became skilled in the trade, as well as working with great speed. However, his 'scoffing' temperament could not long be suppressed and when he takes his master's words far too literally, after being told to 'whip' the sleeves on a gown, the pair part company and Robin absconds again. The youth then has a dream in which his true parentage is disclosed to him: he receives a scroll that informs him that King Oberon is his father (see earlier) and that he has inherited from him his magical, fairy powers:

> "By nature, thou hast cunning shifts
> Which Ile increase with other gifts.
> Wish what thou wilt, thou shalt it have;
> And for to vex both foole and knave,
> Thou hast the power to change thy shape…"

Robin is able to change his appearance and to conjure items out of glamour. These powers are not to be used frivolously, though. Oberon counsels his son as follows:

> "See none thou harm'st but knaves and queanes,
> But love thou those that honest be,
> And helpe them in necessity."

Then, with a promise that he'll meet Oberon in fairyland in due course, Robin sets out into the world to fulfil his mission. A series of adventures and incidents follow, in which the boy enacts his father's instructions. A country fellow who is rude and abrupt is punished by Robin taking the form of a horse and dumping him in a pool. A young woman and her lover are saved from the lecherous designs of her uncle by means of Robin's ploys. A pub landlord who cheats his customers is exposed; a rapist is interrupted; a usurer is scared into becoming a generous man.

Robin repeatedly protects the vulnerable and the poor. He is also lauded for the help he gives to farmers and their labourers by breaking hemp, bolting flour, dressing flax and spinning. He works prodigiously, getting through the tasks in half the time it would take the human servants, and "hee was excellent in everything." Moreover, he sought no reward: as with all hobs and brownies, a gift of clothes would drive him away.

However, Robin is not entirely consistent: whilst he generally defends virtue and constancy, in one incident in the *Mad Pranks* he deliberately sets out to seduce a weaver's wife and to humiliate her husband. In addition, his mocking nature, which had revealed itself during his childhood, cannot be denied. Purely for amusement, Robin will appear as "a walking fire" to lead night-time travellers off the road; he also walks town streets at night, knocking on doors and running away, or posing as a chimney sweep and then disappearing as soon as he's offered work. These rather vexing activities were accompanied by mildly salacious songs, full of suggestive references to maidens' chimneys and honey pots.

Lastly, Robin attended a wedding in the guise of a fiddler and entertained the company before resorting to his usual trying tricks – he blew out the candles, kissed the pretty girls, pinched others and started fights between them and set all the men present to brawling by punching them in the dark. Lastly, when the celebration posset was served at the end of the meal, Robin changed himself into a bear and scared all the party away so he could have the drink to himself. The coarse humour of the prose life is typified by the conclusion to the wedding feast: "The feare that the guests were in did cause such a smell, that the bridegroom did call for perfumes and, instead of a posset, he was faine to make use of cold beere." All these activities are marked by Robin's traditional cry of "Ho! Ho! Ho!"

At last, as promised, Robin met with his father again and visited fairyland, where Oberon "did shew him many secrets, which hee never did open to the world." In both the prose and ballad lives, Robin danced until dawn with the fairies to the sound of bagpipes played by Tom Thumb. In the prose version, however, an extra scene is included in which the fairies of Oberon's court introduce themselves; these are Pinch, Patch, Gull, Grim and Sib and they describe how they indulge in such typical fairy exploits as punishing bad servants and stealing children. Each fairy concludes her account of herself with a short rhyme that reinforces the prevailing moral code within which Robin was seen to operate. For example, fairy Pinch sings:

"To the good I doe no harme,
But cover them and keepe them warme:
Sluts and slovens doe I pinch
And make them in their beds to winch."

Indeed, these five faes might even be seen as manifestations of traits in Robin's own character, expostulating in detail upon certain aspects of his behaviour.

In addition to these two life stories, we have a number of other texts dedicated to Robin Goodfellow. *The Pranks of Puck* is a song that some have attributed to Ben Jonson. It is a brief summary of Robin's antics (further condensing what was described in the *Mad Pranks*), spoken by him in the capacity of an emissary from Oberon, sent to view the nightly sports on earth:

"What revel rout,
Is kept about

In every corner where I go,
I will o'ersee
And merry be,
And make good sport with ho, ho ho!"[21]

In lines clearly inspired by Shakespeare, Mad Robin can fly "more swift than lightning ... about this airy welkin." He acts as a will of the wisp, misleading nocturnal travellers with a "counterfeited voice." He shapeshifts; he performs domestic and agricultural chores; he rewards those who see the fairies dancing but keep quiet about it; he helps the needy with interest-free loans of the sums they require. Conversely, Robin punishes lazy housemaids by pinching them and pulling them naked out of bed; he causes squabbles amongst gossips and frees animals from poachers' traps. Everything in the human world is a potential source of amusement to Robin in this account – even the swapping of changeling elves for new born babies in their cradles.

In 1613 Samuel Rowlands composed a moralistic text titled *More Knaves Yet? The Knaves of Spades and Diamonds*. This included a section on 'Ghoastes and Goblins' in which he reflected upon a fairy belief that he felt was, by then, waning.

"Amongst the rest was a Good Fellow devil,
So cal'd in kindness, cause he did no evil,
Knowne by the name of Robin (as we heare)
And that his eyes as broad as sawcers were..."

Rowlands continued by enumerating Robin's activities. He would visit homes at night, cleaning the kitchens and dairies, but punishing lazy servants. Whilst inclined to see him as a remnant of Popish superstition, the author still judged Puck favourably:

"'Twas a mad Robin that did divers pranckes,
For which with some good cheare they gave him thankes,

---

21 For the full text, see my *Fayerie* (2020).

> And that was all the kindness he expected
> With gaine (it seemes) he was not much infected
> But as that time is past, that Robin's gone..."

Having mourned the passing of the hobgoblin, Rowlands went on to complain about the 'Bad fellows' who then infested England, burgling houses in the night and disturbing the peace.

Puck's Pranks on Twelfth Day was published in 1655 and seems to be a late example of the genre.[22] A "mad merry company" has met together to celebrate twelfth night when "Robbin Goodfellow" appears amongst them and immediately disrupts the party. He provokes a punch-up amongst the men and pinches a woman's buttocks, which only serves to worsen the fighting at the festivities.

This last example accentuates some of the qualities that seem to have made Robin so popular. He had an earthy sense of humour, being devoted to crude practical jokes and rough treatment. Boxed ears and dunks in ponds were as sophisticated as Robin got, but with these japes he dealt out a sort of simple, practical justice. Robin could work hard, as well as drink hard, and he liked wenches and laughter. The key aspect of his character was that he operated within a strict moral code. As it said in the *Mad Pranks,* "he [would] continually practice himself in honest mirth, never doing hurt to any that were cleanly and honest minded." Elsewhere, we are assured that "Robin always did helpe those that suffered wrong, and never would hurt any but those that did wrong to others."

At this point, it may be worth remarking how Robin often shared key traits of his persona with other faery beings. He would often appear as a horse to carry off miscreants, in this respect resembling various supernatural beasts such as the colt-pixy of Hampshire and Dorset, the Scottish kelpie and the Highland water-horse. We just now heard of his 'saucer eyes,' a feature shared with many of the black dogs that haunt the

---

22 *Mercurius Fumigosus, or the Smoking Nocturnall*, no. 32, January 3rd–10th, 1655.

highways of England. Lastly, his ability to change his shape, becoming (amongst other things) a disabled beggar, a soldier, a young woman, a fox, a hare, an owl, a frog, a dog and a tree, associates Robin with many of the bogles, boggarts and brags of northern England. Nonetheless, this shape-shifting was one of his defining features, leading poet Edward Guilpin to refer to him as "The Proteus Robin-goodfellow of change ...".[23]

Through his willingness to undertake hard physical work, his emotional sympathy with the downtrodden, and his preference for simple pleasures, Robin Goodfellow seems to have been adopted by the English working classes as a champion.

THE NATURE & HABITS OF ROBIN GOODFELLOW

The literary lives of Robin Goodfellow attest to his fame and popularity, but he was firmly embedded in English culture long before they appeared, and the details that the plays, masques and pamphlets provide about Robin confirm, or are supplemented by, a host of other sources that concern or mention him.

Robin has been called "the most famous and the most esteemed of all the spirits and supernatural beings who haunted England."[24] It will be noted that the writer here did *not* call Robin a fairy. He only really became associated with fairykind through the intervention of Shakespeare, who integrated him fully within the fairy court and deprived him of his solitary, sovereign status. Before the *Dream,* he was understood to be an independently existing sprite – and one whose exact nature was open to debate. Robin was related in some way to the nightmare and incubus (as we have just seen),[25] to the will of the wisp,

---

23 Guilpin, *Skialetheia, or a Shadowe of Truth in certaine Epigrams and Satyres*, 1598, 'Satyra Sexta.' On the other faery beasts mentioned, see my *Beyond Faery*, 2020.

24 Minor White Latham, *The Elizabethan Fairies*, 1930, 220.

25 See too William Baldwin, *Beware the Cat*, 1584, 22 & William Cartwright, *The Ordinary* 1651, III, 1.

to ghosts, to demons, to domestic spirits and, even, to human beings. The extent of the uncertainty about Robin's exact nature emerges at the end of the *Ballad of Robin Goodfellow*, when the narrator states:

> "Some call him Robin Goodfellow, Hobgoblin or mad Crisp,
> And some again doe terme him oft by name of Will the
> Wispe,
> But call him by what name you list, I have studied on my
> pillow,
> I think the best name he deserves, is Robin Goodfellow."

This stanza uses just a handful of the names that were applied to Robin, each implying a slightly different conception of his nature. He was also called Pug Robin, Lob-Lie-by-the-Fire, Lubbar Fiend, lubber and Hodgepoke.[26]

Some of Robin's associations have already been noted. Certainly, church influence had for some centuries been linking him with the devil. This is explicit in one manuscript that refers to "Robin, eclyped Imp of Hell or divell" and it's seen too in the role given to him in a number of plays – for example, in *Grim the Collier of Croydon*, he's called a "country-devil."[27] Robert Burton, in the *Anatomy of Melancholy*, grouped hobgoblins and Robin together as being amongst the bigger sort of terrestrial devils.[28] Furthermore, it should be noted that, in the later Middle Ages, 'pouke' was another name for Satan, so that in *Piers Plowman* Langland used "the pook's pinfold" as a synonym for Hell.[29]

Elsewhere, Robin was described as being human. He has a human mother, of course, in the two lives we have examined already. In the 1640 ballad, *A Monstrous Shape*, he is said to

---

26 Names taken from Butler, *Hudibras*; Beaumont, *Knight of the Burning Pestle*; Milton, *L'Allegro; Misognus* and Thomas Churchyard, *A Handful of Gladsome Verses*.

27 Bod. MS Ashmole 36–37, no.317, 306; see too Ben Jonson, *The Devil is an Ass* and Anon, *Wily Beguiled*.

28 Burton, *Anatomy*, 1621, 124.

29 Langland, *Piers Plowman*, Passus 16, line 263; see too the 13th century Middle English *Sinners Beware!* and *St. Gregory*.

have been a man who was abducted by the fairy queen – just like Thomas the Rhymer, whilst in the play, *Wily Beguiled*, he's a witch's son. Robin seems to have been the leader, patron or even deity of English witches: those in Somerset cried out 'Robin' when summoning their master to a sabbat.[30]

Several sources describe Robin as a kind of bogie, as a bugbear or a bull-beggar. In *Wily Beguiled*, for instance, Robin declares that he'll "play the Bugbeare wheresoe'er I come." He'll don his flashing red nose and flaming face and set about scaring people like a "scarbabe" [a scarecrow] or a "Hellish Hag or damned fiend."[31] Interestingly, in Shadwell's play *The Lancashire Witches*, the character Puck is described as "an imp like a black shock" – a 'shock' or 'shug' being a supernatural beast or bogie taking the form of a black dog or similar animal.[32]

The longstanding consensus, nonetheless, was that Robin Goodfellow was a member of, or linked to, or was to be grouped with, the family of hobthrusts and hobgoblins. This was the case from at least the later fifteenth century. His relationship to the pucks and pixies was definitely known, but the detail was rather less certain: hence, for example, when George Gascoigne listed types of fairy being in his play *The Buggbears*, he enumerated "puckes, puckerels... and Robin Goodfellow." They seem to have had features in common, whilst not being identical.[33]

All in all, therefore, we may summarise Robin Goodfellow as an "honest, plain country spirit." He was not subject to any sort of authority – either of a fairy monarch nor even of a wider fairy family. He operated autonomously, behaving as he wished and going wherever he chose – but his preference was for woodlands and rural cottages and farms. As he said of himself in Jonson's

---

30 Lewis Spence, *Fairy Tradition in Britain*, 19.

31 *Wily Beguiled*, 1606, line 479.

32 See too Scot, *The Discoverie of Witchcraft*, 'To the Reader' and *Grim the Collier of Croydon*. On the black dogs and shugs, see my *Beyond Faery*, 2020.

33 Gascoigne, *Buggbears*, Act III, line 58; see too Spenser, *Epithalamion*, lines 341–343, *Tarlton's News Out of Purgatory*, 1588, 55 & 222, or George Munday, *Fidele & Fidelio*, line 566; *The Masque at Coleorton*.

play, *Love Restored,* his preferred activities were such things as shoeing wild mares and roasting robin redbreasts.

During the fifteenth and sixteenth centuries, when he entered the literary and historical records, it is clear that English people were absolutely convinced of the reality of Robin, an "illusion" that Reginald Scot repeatedly scorned and criticised in *The Discovery of Witchcraft.*[34] Accordingly, the details of Robin's appearance were well-established. He was a large, broad male, of "bigger bulke and voice." Because of his solid frame, he couldn't enter properties through keyholes or cracks in window panes like the fairies could – he had to go in through the door like any man.[35] He was often described as being dressed in a tight leather or calf-skin suit and his face and hands were russet in colour (like a brownie). Sometimes, though, Robin wore no garments at all – because he was so hairy. In Jonson's *Sad Shepherd* of 1641 he's called Puck Hairy; in the play *Misognus* he's likened to a "tumbling bear." Earlier, we read that Robin was able to turn himself into a bear and another source makes a similar comparison when Robin is in the guise of Lob Lie by the Fire. Joseph Ritson recorded in his *Dissertation of Fairies* (published in 1831) that a female relative had described Lob resting after his labours and "lying before the fire like a great rough hurgin bear." The word 'hurgin' probably should be pronounced with a soft 'g,' indicating that it is a dialect version of 'urchin,' a hedgehog, and so indicates the spiky and unkempt nature of Lob's fur.[36]

Robin's character and habits were also widely known. His prevailing qualities, those which go very far to explain the popular love for him, were his pleasant disposition – his amiability, sense of humour, his love of jests and pranks – and his well-intentioned and good-natured meddling in human

---

34 Scot, *Discoverie*, 1584, 'To the Reader;' Book IV, c.19; Book VII chapters 2 & 15; Book VIII, c.1; Book XVI, c.7;

35 Warner, *The Shepherd's Dream;* Jonson, *Love Restored*.

36 *Misognus* I, 3; see also Jonson, *Love Restored*; Ritson, *Dissertation*, 22–23. In *Wily Beguiled*, 1606, Robin appears in an "ougly uncouth shape" in order to scare a cruel father.

affairs. *Tell-Trothes New-Yeares Gift,* published in 1593, termed him a "merry mate" who corrected manners and made servants diligent. Robin liked good company and good ale, hence Thomas Churchyard, referring to him as Hodgepoke, said he "would come and drink carows" [that is, toasts, as in carousing]. When, as we saw earlier, he was condemned as an "Imp of Hell," this was, it transpired, for the modest sins of going drinking and living an "uncivill life."[37] Robin was renowned for his laughter and his tricks; he would plague people, causing inconvenience and annoyance, perhaps, but never doing any real harm.[38]

Thomas Churchyard also called Robin a 'lout' because of his rough and robust humour. Although he was ostensibly describing Puck, Shakespeare illustrated this with his account of pulling away stools from under old women and such like. Robin was described in *The Cobler of Canterbury* as a "ruffler" – a swaggering, roistering fellow; this side of his character was further emphasised in William Haughton's play, *Grim the Collier of Croydon.* Tired of the city, Robin resolves to go into the country; he changes shape so that he can scare people as he goes and he plans to survive by stealing cream from bowls and bacon from flitches.[39]

Mad and merry pranks was what Robin was all about-most typically when he behaved in ways that blurred the lines between the hob and the Will of the Wisp. So it is that Thomas Heywood has Hobson in *If You Know Not Me* reminisce in these terms:

> "Now I remember mine old grandmother
> Would talk of fairies and hobgoblins,
> That would lead milk maids over hedge and ditch

---

37 Churchyard, *A Handful of Gladsome Verses*; Bod. MS Ashmole 36–37, no.317, 306.

38 Collier, *A Book of Roxburghe Ballads*, 1847, 35; Rowlands, *More Knaves Yet?* 'Of Ghoastes and Goblins;' *Tarleton's News out of Purgatorie*, 1590; *Love Restored.*

39 *Cobler of Canterburie*, 1608, 'Robin Goodfellow's Epistle;' Haughton, *Grim the Collier*, 1605, Act IV, scene 1; *Wily Beguiled*, Act IV, scene 1.

> Make them milk their neighbours' kine
> And, ten to one, this Robin Goodfellow
> Hath led me up and down the madman's maze."[40]

Protestant divine William Tyndale used very similar words when he described how the failure to teach people how to understand the scriptures meant that the gospel could "become a maze unto them, in which they wander as in a mist, or (as we say) led by Robin Goodfellow, that they cannot come to the right way, no, though they turn their caps …"[41]

As poet Thomas Heywood understood, Robin was also very commonly encountered as a domestic type of spirit and was closely associated with people's homes:

> "Pugs and Hobgoblins. Their dwellings bee
> In corners of old houses least frequented …
> Robin Goodfellow some, some call them fairies."

In Heywood's opinion, Robin's greatest habit was making noise, upturning furniture and utensils, and disrupting the orderly functioning of the household, undoing all the hard work done by the servants. William Tyndale reported the same, making a strange comparison: "The Pope is akin to Robin Goodfellow, who sweeps the house, washes the dishes and purges all by night; but, when day comes, there is nothing found clean."[42]

Margaret Cavendish, Duchess of Newcastle, also agreed that the hobs' presence in homes seldom brought real benefits:

> "these spirits be a dangerous band of whifflers [men of inconstant opinion], and, like our Robin Good-fellows, will play their legerdemain tricks, scudding here and there in a trice…"[43]

---

40 Heywood, *If You Know Not Me, You Know Nobody*, 1605.

41 Tyndale, *Exposition on the First Gospel of St John.*

42 Heywood, *Hierarchie of Blessed Angels*, 574; Tyndale, *The Obedience of the Christian Man.*

43 Cavendish, *Pastime of the Queen of Fairy*; see too Anon., *Lady Alimony*, 1659, Act III, scene 5; *Roxburghe Ballads*, vol.2, 'The Devil and the Scold.'

Most others (his likely beneficiaries) viewed Robin more benignly, and believed that he would grind corn, malt and mustard, cut wood, thresh grain, bake and brew beer, clean the house and churn butter. Thus, for Ben Jonson, he was:

> "the honest, plain country spirit and harmless… he that sweeps the hearth and the house clean, riddles for the country maid and does all the other drudgery whilst they are at hot cockles [a game] …"[44]

The fact that Robin undertook the servants' work, so that they had leisure time to play games with their companions, doubtless contributed to his popularity amongst the labouring classes.[45]

Without doubt, Robin was consistently depicted as an extremely busy and hard-working sprite.[46] Because of his commitment to labouring at heavy chores, he was regularly described, or was seen in illustrations, carrying implements symbolic of his functions: a candle (representative of his role as a Jack o' Lantern or Kit with the Canstick) and either a broom or flail.[47] Along with his trademark mocking laugh, his sweeping made Robin unmistakeable to contemporary readers and audiences.

We must recognise, though, that the drudgery that Robin undertook was *not* performed purely out of a kindly spirit. As Reginald Scot recorded, there was a "standing fee" for his work, a "messe of bread and milk."[48] Like Queen Mab, Robin had a particular taste for dairy produce and many authors alluded to this. For Ben Jonson, then, he was the epitome of the "coarse and country fairy/ That doth haunt the Hearth and Dairy." He was often found "amongst the creame-bowles and milke-pans"

---

44 Jonson, *Love Restored*, 1612; see too Robert Burton, *Anatomy of Melancholy*, 124; Scot, *Discoverie of Witchcraft*, Book IV, c.10.

45 See too S. Harsenet, *A Declaration of Egregious Popish Impostures*, 1603, 134.

46 For example, *Grim the Collier of Croydon* (1662).

47 See, for instance, *Love Restored* or Scot, *Discoverie of Witchcraft*, Book IV, c.10.

48 Scot, *Discoverie*, Book IV, c.10.

keeping dairies clean and tidy and seeking only "some fresh cheese hire" in return. Thomas Churchyard also made reference to this preference:

> "Rude Robin Goodfellow, the lout,
> Would skime the milk bowls all.
> And search the cream pots too,
> For which poore milke maid weeps,
> God wot what such mad gests will doe:
> When people soundly sleeps."[49]

Lastly, "Honest Puck" was not only a friend to dutiful domestic servants; he also, as we saw previously, was a great matchmaker, who could not resist interfering in the love affairs of humans. Shakespeare seems to have been well aware of this propensity, for in *Midsummer Night's Dream* his Puck takes pity on the jilted Hermia, exclaiming:

> "Here she comes, curst and sad;
> Cupid is a knavish lad,
> Thus to make poor females sad."

In reality, it was Puck, rather than Cupid, whose interventions had caused the lovers to fall out in the first place, but he also remedies the tiff.[50]

In summary, then, Robin's jollity, his practical jokes, his sense of fairness implemented through rough justice, his work ethic, his capacity for good ale, all commended him to the English. He was well-known and well-loved, which is why Shakespeare chose to incorporate him into a play. However, in doing that, linking him with the fairies and renaming him, the playwright also initiated the decline of one of English fairy-lore's greatest characters.

---

49 *Tarlton's News out of Purgatory*, 1588, 55 & 222; Jonson, *Oberon the Fairy*, 1611; Samuel Rowlands, 'Of Ghoastes and Goblins,' in *More Knaves Yet?*, 1613; Churchyard, *A Handful of Gladsome Verses*, 1592; *Grim the Collier of Croydon*; Harsenet, *A Declaration of Egregious Popish Impostures*, 1603, 134.

50 *Midsummer Night's Dream*, III, 2; also *Love Restore, Grim the Collier of Croydon* and *Wily Beguiled*, 1606.

SHAKESPEARE'S PUCK

Shakespeare very probably knew about pucks from the stories he heard during his boyhood in Warwickshire. They provided him with the essentials of his character's behaviour and abilities.

Puck is first addressed by a fairy he meets as a "lob of spirits" (another expression for a hobgoblin) but she then realises who he is – an identification he readily acknowledges. Puck's role as jester to the court is spelled out, along with the traditional activities of the puck. He plays pranks on maids and housewives and acts like a will o' the wisp, 'pixie-leading' nocturnal travellers out of their way:[51]

> *"Fairy –*
> Either I mistake your shape and making quite,
> Or else you are that shrewd and knavish sprite
> Call'd Robin Goodfellow: are not you he
> That frights the maidens of the villagery;
> Skim milk, and sometimes labour in the quern
> And bootless make the breathless housewife churn;
> And sometime make the drink to bear no barm;
> Mislead night-wanderers, laughing at their harm?
> Those that Hobgoblin call you and sweet Puck,
> You do their work, and they shall have good luck:
> Are not you he?
> *Puck –*
> Thou speak'st aright;
> I am that merry wanderer of the night.
> I jest to Oberon and make him smile
> When I a fat and bean-fed horse beguile,
> Neighing in likeness of a filly foal:
> And sometime lurk I in a gossip's bowl,
> In very likeness of a roasted crab,
> And when she drinks, against her lips I bob
> And on her wither'd dewlap pour the ale.

---

51 Act II, 1.

The wisest aunt, telling the saddest tale,
Sometime for three-foot stool mistaketh me;
Then slip I from her bum, down topples she,
And 'tailor' cries, and falls into a cough;
And then the whole quire hold their hips and laugh,
And waxen in their mirth and sneeze and swear
A merrier hour was never wasted there."

It should be noted that this scene seems to imply that Puck is known to the fairies, but that is not one of them – reflecting the problems of defining his nature mentioned earlier. He is referred to here as Robin Goodfellow and, indeed, at one point in the play he even uses Robin's traditional exclamation of "Ho, Ho, Ho!"[52]

Despite the foregoing tally of his solo activities, in *Midsummer Night's Dream* Puck's function is to be a "mad spirit" who runs errands for Oberon, assisting him with his charms and plots. It seems that he has magical powers independent of those of the fairy king, but that he exercises them at the king's command. Puck can throw his voice and become invisible, he can conjure up fogs (like the Cornish pixies) and he can change the shape of others (as well as his own), as when he gives Bottom an ass's head. He can travel "swifter than the wind" or "an arrow from a Tartar's bow" and could "put a girdle round the world in forty minutes."

Unfortunately, in carrying out the king's orders, Puck mistakes his targets and creates even greater confusion and nuisance. In his responses to this, it seems to be revealed that Oberon lacks full confidence in his servant's abilities. He suspects Puck of being either negligent or of indulging wilful knaveries – although, when matters go right, the fairy king is also prepared to address his servant as 'good' and 'gentle.'

At the very close of the play, Robin also performs a theatrical role as the chorus, in which he summarises and concludes the action. Whilst doing so, though, he still affirms his essential nature. It is night time, the elves are "frolic" through the human

---

52 Act III, 2.

palace and Puck has been sent "with broom before/ To sweep the dust behind the door" in order to bring good fortune to the newly wed couples.[53]

Shakespeare's Puck was so successful because he incorporated all the characteristics of Robin Goodfellow as well as many of the traits of the fairies as well. Minor White Latham has called Puck a "happy, frisky fairy," a being distinct from Robin and who eventually eclipsed him in fame.[54]

PUCK & ROBIN AFTER *THE DREAM*

Puck's fundamental nature as a hobgoblin is preserved in a number of works by Ben Jonson. In *The Devil is an Ass* of 1616 the character Pug is identical with Robin Goodfellow and plays the tricks we would expect of his kind: he stales yeast, sours cream, stops butter churning and "other dim tricks."[55] In *The Sad Shepherd* (1641) he appears as a familiar sprite called Puck-Hairy but, like the Puck of the *Dream,* he is a lackey, performing a witch's errands and dashing about a forest "like a Goblin." We may note that Puck's nature is still not fully resolved: he behaves in the same way as a goblin without actually being one.

In Drayton's *Nimphidia,* Puck is once more made subservient to Oberon – yet he is at the same time unequivocally a traditional sprite, "which most men call/ Hobgoblin," and he utters the "Ho, Ho, Ho" typical of his kind. He is reported to perform the functions assigned to him by folklore:

> "This Puck seemes but a dreaming dolt,
> Still walking like a ragged Colt,
> And oft out of a Bush doth bolt,
> Of purpose to deceive us.
> And leading us makes us to stray,
> Long Winters nights out of the way,

---

53 Act V, 2.
54 Latham, *The Elizabethan Fairies,* 220.
55 Act I, 1.

And when we stick in mire and clay,
Hob doth with laughter leave us."

These traits notwithstanding, Drayton's Puck is still at the beck and call of his master. He is ordered to fetch unfaithful Queen Mab dead or alive and to bring too her lover's head. He promises to obey with the utmost speed and devotion and there is a great danger he will succeed, especially as he is also endowed with "a sharpe and piercing sight." Luckily for the queen, the fairy Nimphidia overhears Oberon and Puck plotting and she casts a spell on the hob that terminates his diligent searching:

"And he was caught as in a Gin;
For as he thus was busie,
A paine he in his Head-peece feeles,
Against a stubbed Tree he reeles,
And up went poore Hobgoblins heeles,
Alas his braine was dizzie."

Despite his own magical powers, the hobgoblin is ensnared by brambles and bogs (his own traps for unwary humans) and, roaring with rage, he alerts the queen to his proximity thereby permitting her to escape with her lover.

Separately from these developments in the character of Puck, Robin Goodfellow was going through his own transformations. Having been the servant of Oberon in the *Dream,* he too appeared more and more as a subservient character. Several playwrights also emphasised the demonic aspect of his character, making Robin a lackey of Satan and – what was worse – not a very effective one.[56] This led, in due course and perfectly logically, to him being cast as a witch's familiar. All these roles diminished the respect in which Robin was held, a trend indicated in the nicknames he was given: Pug, Pucky, Pucklin, Puckling. He became a figure of fun – no longer the life and soul of the party.[57]

---

56 Jonson, *The Devil is an Ass; Grim the Collier of Croydon.*
57 Middleton, *The Witch*; Heywood, *The Late Lancashire Witches*, 1634; Jonson, *The Sad Shepherd*, 1637; Shadwell, *The Lancashire Witches*, 1682.

As a consequence of the changes to Robin in the late seventeenth century, he virtually disappeared from popular consciousness. However, the Puck character that Shakespeare created has proved so memorable and so attractive that he has persisted into the modern age. Thomas Hood imagined meeting him in *The Plea of the Midsummer Fairies*. "Quaint Puck the Antic" oddly arrives at the faery gathering along with "Robin Goodfellow, that merry swain." He is a tiny, but a jolly, soul:

> "But Puck was seated on a spider's thread,
> That hung between two branches of a briar,
> And 'gan to swing and gambol, heels o'er head,
> Like any Southwark tumbler on a wire."

As in *Midsummer Night's Dream,* his role is to be a jester, keeping spirits high. The same is true in *The Legend of Puck the Fairy* by Thomas Moore (1779–1852) and, a century later, Arthur Peterson portrayed Puck in precisely the same manner, calling him "merry wanderer" and "trickster."[58] Eugene Lee-Hamilton (1845–1907) also picked up on the idea of a diminutive Puck who could hide in hazelnut shells and described his burial by a mole and four dormice.[59]

Puck also became a favourite in the visual arts, primarily because he offered opportunities to paint faun-like beings and because his scenes promised action and humour. An early representation is by William Blake: *Oberon, Titania and Puck, with Fairies Dancing* (1785). As is typical of Blake, the king is rendered as a medieval English monarch, with long hair and beard, whilst the other figures are classical in appearance; Puck himself is a balletic youth crowned with ivy. Henry Fuseli's *Robin Goodfellow, or Puck,* of 1787–90 looks rather more like what we might expect, he is a rather muscular and coarse male with bat wings. Sir Joshua Reynold's *Puck,* painted in 1789, was a great

---

58 *Halloween, 1916.* See too Madison Cawein, *On Midsummer Night, Wood Dreams, The World of Faery* and *Fairies*; Thomas Hood, *Parental Ode*; E.J. Rupert Atkinson, *The Flight of Puck.*

59 Lee-Hamilton, *The Death of Puck*, published 1916.

success when exhibited. The subject is portrayed as a plump, naked baby with pointed ears. He is sat alone in a wood, playing with flowers he's picked, but his generally infantile appearance is belied by a very mischievous expression. Daniel Maclise's *Faun and Fairies* of about 1834 might show us Reynold's Puck grown up. The faun is a muscular figure playing pan-pipes whilst naked, dancing fairies swirl around him. In 1837 Scottish painter David Scott produced a very distinctive image of *Puck Fleeing Before the Dawn*. His figure may also be derived from Reynolds': he is a nude boy with moth wings who's flying through the air with his legs hugged against his body. The use of faun or Pan-like features in some of these paintings may, in fact, reflect the lack of certainty about the true identity and appearance of Puck which I described earlier. Given his somewhat formless character, modelling him upon a classical precedent may have seemed very attractive to artists and audiences.

Richard Dadd's *Puck* of 1841 perpetuated the trend for him to be portrayed as small and childlike – in this case, he is seated upon a toadstool. Sir Noel Paton seems to have been drawn repeatedly to scenes featuring Puck in Shakespeare's play. *Puck and the Fairies* (1850) finds him relaxing with a group of mainly grotesque figures. He leans on a mushroom, a robust and not very handsome male with an incongruous pair of butterfly wings. In *Puck and Titania: A Scene from Midsummer Night's Dream,* the same rather rough and ugly male, with exaggerated donkey ears, chats with a graceful, naked queen. *Puck and the Fairy* depicts the first scene in which the fairies appear in the play, with Puck presented as a solid male figure in a red cape and hood, apparently about to molest the surprised and naked fay; she clasps her long hair about her for some kind of protection. In 1853, minor artist Edward Hopley painted *Puck and the Moth*, reverting again to a vision of a putto-like boy, wearing a flower as a cap, to represent his main subject. That said, he is using a thorn like a lance to attack the helpless insect, so he is plainly not as innocent as he seems. Lastly, another infantile Puck appears in John George Naish's *Midsummer Fairies*, exhibited in 1856;

in this picture, though, the boy is shrunk to almost microscopic dimensions, permitting him to ride on a moth's back.

Paintings of Puck seems to have fallen from favour by the middle of the nineteenth century; we do not encounter him again in art until well into the twentieth century. Arthur Rackham's Puck, drawn to illustrate a 1930 edition of the play, is another boy, this time dressed in a spotted suit with a pointy hat, and, when Peter Blake came to paint the character several decades later, he also chose to depict a young male. *Puck, Peaseblossom, Cobweb, Moth and Mustardseed*, which Blake started in 1969, finds Puck along with a number of tinier, winged child-fairies. They seem to be in a suburban garden and Puck is shown as a naked boy, regarding observers with a cheerful, friendly expression and (apparently) the face of early 1960s rock and roll crooner Del Shannon – doubtless a homage by Blake to one of the idols of his teens. Another study of Puck by Blake from 1988 again depicts him as a smiling boy, set against the backdrop of a large country garden.

Returning to the puck's career in literature, we find that the influence of Shakespeare – whilst pervasive – was not overpowering. The poem *Lubber Fiend* by Madison Julius Cawein (1865–1914) made it very clear that Robin's traditional character had *not* been forgotten, even in the late nineteenth century:

"In the woods, not long ago,
Met with Robin Goodfellów;
First we heard his horse-like laugh
In an ivy-bush nearby;
Then we saw him, like a calf,
Or a frisky colt, just fly
Kicking high his frantic heels,
Squealing as a scared pig squeals.

Snorting, baaing, neighing too,
Through the woods he fairly flew;
Father followed him, but he

122

Couldn't catch him long of limb
As a grasshopper, you see,
There's no man could capture him:
Then, besides, his colour's green,
So he's rarely ever seen.

Often when you're in the woods,
Just a-walking with your moods,
And not thinking; listening how
Still it is, right near your head
Breaks the bellow of a cow
And you drop scared nearly gone:
That's old Robin you can't see
'Cause he's coloured like a tree.

And I've heard he calls and calls
In the woods for help, or falls,
Like an urchin, from a tree:
You jump up and shout and run
But there's nothing there to see;
Just a snickering as of fun
in the thicket, or somewhere,
And you're madder than a hare.

Sometimes in dark woods a light
Flashes in your eyes, as bright
As a firefly after rain;
And your eyes are dazzled so
That you shut them look again
Nothing's there. That's Goodfellów,
With his jack-o'-lantern; see?
Hiding in some hollow tree.

These are pranks he plays on men
When he feels all right; but when
He is out of humour, well!
Better keep away! he'll harm:
Leads you with a heifer's bell,

Or horn-lantern, to some farm,
You suppose; but 't isn't! no!
Some old bog in which you go.

Sometimes he's called Puck, they say:
And it was the other day
Father read me from a book
That some people call him Lob
One who haunts the ingle-nook,
Or sits humped upon the hob
Whistling up the chimney-flue
Till the kettle whistles too.

He's the Lubber Fiend, that sweeps
Ashes in your face and creeps
Under cracks when north winds howl;
Hides behind the closet door
And peeps at you, like an owl,
Bumps you shrieking on the floor;
And at night he rides a mare
Round your bed and everywhere.

And he teases dogs that doze
By the fire; and, I suppose,
They must see him in their dreams
When they snarl and glare o'erhead:
And it's he, or so it seems,
Tumbles children out of bed,
Wakes the house and makes a fuss;
For he's awful mischievous.

That's what I heard father say,
And I know it's true. Some day
I'm a-going to be a boy
Just like Robin; romp and shout,
And kick up my heels for joy,
And scare people round about;
Just play tricks on everyone.

Don't you think it would be fun?
Take an old cow-horn, that's harsh
As a frog that haunts the marsh,
And when folks are in their beds
Blow it at the windowsill
Till they cover up their heads;
And when all again is still,
Hear them wonder what it was
That was making all that fuss.

Or I'll make a pumpkin face;
Light, and hide it in some place
Where are bushes; and when men
Come along I'll grunt and groan
Like an old pig in its pen;
When they run I'll throw a stone,
Or just vanish; and they'll say
'What was that, I wonder? eh?'

It would be a lot of fun,
Wouldn't it? to make folks run;
Jumping at them from the dark
Like a big black dog, oh my!
It would be the greatest lark!
Wonder why it is that I
Can't grow up at once like you
And do things I'd like to do?

This entire poem is a spirited reassertion of the genuine nature
of Robin. It might even be described as a modern verse rendition
of the seventeenth century *Ballad of Robin Goodfellow*.

Rudyard Kipling's *Puck of Pook Hill*, published in 1908, was
a further belated assertion of the original or authentic character
of Puck. The child heroes of the stories, Dan and Una, have
been acting scenes from *Midsummer Night's Dream* in a meadow
near their Sussex home. It is Midsummer's Eve and it turns out
that performing that play three times in a row at that magical

time of year, *and* in a field marked by a fairy ring, can have only one effect: they summon up Puck, "a small, brown, broad-shouldered, pointy-eared person with a snub nose, slanting blue eyes and a grin that ran right across his freckled face." Kipling's description immediately confronts us with Robin as the Tudors and Stuarts would have recognised him.

Puck's appearance is surprising, but not alarming, as he seems a friendly fellow. All the same, he warns the pair that doing what they had just done a few hundred years earlier could have been a different matter. They were sitting at the foot of Pook's Hill and, in the past, they would "have had all the People of the Hills out like bees in June." Sadly, though, "the Hills are empty now, and all the People of the Hills are gone. I'm the only one left. I'm Puck, the oldest Old Thing in England, very much at your service if – if you care to have anything to do with me." The children do care to do so, and the three quickly become friends.

Puck (who's also called Robin Goodfellow, Nick o' Lincoln and Lob-lie-by-the-Fire) shares the children's picnic with them, assuring them that he has no objection to salt:

> "'That'll show you the sort of person I am. Some of us' – he went on, with his mouth full – 'couldn't abide Salt, or Horse-shoes over a door, or Mountain-ash berries, or Running Water, or Cold Iron, or the sound of Church Bells. But I'm Puck!'"

The three sit together and Puck quickly sketches out the history of the fairies in England. He explains to them that:

> "The People of the Hills have all left. I saw them come into Old England and I saw them go. Giants, trolls, kelpies, brownies, goblins, imps; wood, tree, mound, and water spirits; heath-people, hill-watchers, treasure-guards, good people, little people, pishogues, leprechauns, night-riders, pixies, nixies, gnomes, and the rest – gone, all gone! I came into England with Oak, Ash and Thorn, and when Oak, Ash

and Thorn are gone I shall go too." [*There's little danger of this, though, as Puck plants acorns every autumn.*]

Puck makes clear a particular point of etiquette, nonetheless. He objects to the word 'fairy' and always says 'People of the Hills.'

> "That's how I feel about saying – that word that I don't say. Besides, what you call them are made-up things the People of the Hills have never heard of – little buzzflies with butterfly wings and gauze petticoats, and shiny stars in their hair, and a wand like a schoolteacher's cane for punishing bad boys and rewarding good ones. I know 'em! ...
>
> Can you wonder that the People of the Hills don't care to be confused with that painty-winged, wand-waving, sugar-and-shake-your-head set of impostors? Butterfly wings, indeed! ... Butterfly-wings! It was Magic – Magic as black as Merlin could make it ... That was how it was in the old days!"

As for Puck himself, his traditional tastes remain intact: "Now, I began as I mean to go on. A bowl of porridge, a dish of milk, and a little quiet fun with the country folk in the lanes was enough for me then, as it is now. I belong here, you see, and I have been mixed up with people all my days. "

After this introduction, Puck proceeds to guide Dan and Una through a history of England. He is still the soul of England, if you like, the spirit of the land and its history and, as such, he is timeless and indestructible.[60]

---

60 Kipling, *Puck of Pook's Hill*, 1908, 'Weland's Sword;' see too *Rewards and Fairies*, 1910.

CHAPTER ELEVEN

Rumpelstiltskin and his Kin

Rumpelstiltskin is *not* a being of British traditional faery lore: he originates in German folklore and was popularised by the brothers Grimm. Nevertheless, he is simply a cousin to very similar faeries in the British Isles and, for this reason, I use him to denote a family of native spirits well-known in native folklore.

THE GRIMMS STORY

The story of Rumpelstilzchen was published by the Grimm brothers in the 1812 edition of *Children's and Household Tales*. It's plot is as follows.

A miller boasts to the king that his daughter can spin straw into gold. The king summons the girl and shuts her in a room in a tower that is filled with straw. She is given a spinning wheel and is ordered to spin the straw into gold by the morning – or she will lose her head. The girl is in despair, but an imp-like creature appears beside her and spins the straw into gold, asking only for her necklace in return. The king is delighted with what he finds the next day, so he locks the miller's daughter in a larger room filled with even more straw so that she can repeat the feat. The imp returns and does the spinning again, this time in exchange for a ring the girl wears. On the third day, the girl is taken to a yet larger room filled with straw; the king promises this time that he will marry her if she can convert it all to gold overnight – otherwise he will execute her. She has nothing valuable left to offer the sprite except to promise that to give him her first-born child. On the basis of this bargain, he spins the straw into gold one final time.

The king marries the miller's daughter, but when their first child is born, the imp returns to claim his promised reward. The young queen offers him all the riches of the kingdom to preserve her baby, but he only wants the infant. Finally, the imp agrees that he will give up his claim if she can guess his name within three days.

Many attempts to guess the name fail, but on the last night the queen wanders into the woods searching for the imp and comes across him outside his cottage, where he is dancing round a fire and singing:

"Tonight, tonight, my plans I make,
Tomorrow, tomorrow, the baby I take.
The queen will never win the game,
For Rumpelstiltskin is my name."

When the imp comes to the queen for a final time, she at first pretends to guess wrongly before finally, and triumphantly, pronouncing his name. When he realises that he has lost his bargain, Rumpelstiltskin falls into a rage and storms off without his prize.

This fairy tale has been reprinted and repeated in numerous children's books over the last two centuries. It is almost universally familiar, but – as we've seen – it is an import.

BRITISH EQUIVALENTS

A number of British faery accounts pair the faeries' spinning skills with a task imposed upon a human that can be both impossible – and fatal – if it's not completed. In many of these stories (as in *Rumpelstiltskin*) it's a cruel human who sets the hopeless task and a fay who helps to complete it.

A good example of this type of tale is the story of Habetrot from the English-Scottish Borders, in which a girl must prove her female skill at the spinning wheel or face some unspecified punishment from her mother. A faery woman named Habetrot (who's been called the patron spirit of spinning) appears and assists the daughter, aided by a team of helpers including a being called Scantlie Mab, who may or may not be related in some ill-defined way to the fairy queen of that name. She is an ugly and deformed old woman, whilst the 'scant' element of her name might be indicative of her diminutive stature. As for the name Habetrot, we shall see that its final element is found in the names of many of the sprites connected to spinning stories, although its significance is uncertain: 'trot' is a dialect word for an old woman, which is highly appropriate to this story, at least. As for the first part, it may derive from 'hob' as in the goblin, it may have the connotations of 'crude' and 'rustic,' or it might be a diminutive, as in 'hobby-horse,' although all these words are ultimately linked etymologically, deriving from a single source.[1]

Unfortunately, this kind of faery assistance isn't always free and disinterested. In the Suffolk tale of *Tom Tit Tot* a girl has to spin a large quantity of yarn overnight or face beheading by the king. The imp Tom Tit Tot helps her on condition that she will belong to him – unless she can accomplish another impossible sounding task and guess his name. Fortunately, she overhears it and is saved.[2] Welsh sprites Sili-go-Dwt and Trwtyn-Tratyn, the Cornish Terry-Top, Scottish Perrifool, Whuppity-Stoorie, Marget Totts, Titty Tod and Fittle-te-trot are all similar characters in British folk tales in which an elf helps with spinning flax or some similar thread and demands a forfeit unless its name is guessed.[3]

Occasionally it's a faery who imposes the impossible spinning task. In one Scottish example a girl is abducted by the *sith* folk under a hillock and is told that she will be held there until she has spun all the wool in a large sack and eaten all the meal in

1   W. Henderson, *Folk-Lore of the Northern Counties*, 258–62.
2   Edward Clodd, *Tom Tit Tot – An Essay on Savage Philosophy*, 1898.
3   For the latter versions, see Robert Chambers, *Popular Rhymes of Scotland*, 1870, 72–77; British Association, *Papers of the Liverpool Meeting*, 1896, 613; *Athenaeum* no.1001, Jan. 2nd 1847, 18.

a huge chest. Despite her diligent efforts, neither diminish, and she faces eternal confinement and labour until another captive soul tells her to rub spit on her left eyelid every morning. Doing as instructed, she is able to reduce the wool and meal until she finally escapes.

The heroine in such stories isn't always saved and isn't always successful, though. In the case of Welsh girl Eilian, she was obliged to become the wife of a faery man and live in Faery forever after she failed to finish the large quantity of wool that he'd demanded she spin. In the Scottish ballad *The Elfin Knight* a human maid is told that the only way she has any hope of marrying the faery knight is to make him a shirt without cut or hem, shaping it without shears and sewing it without needle and thread. This impossible task is combined with a comparable counter-demand to sow and harvest a field subject to unachievable conditions. Needless to say, the shirt is never made and the girl doesn't get the boy.

A number of very characteristic fairy traits are incorporated in these stories. We find their superior skills in certain crafts – which can be conveyed to humans, but at a cost. We are reminded of the fairies' ability to listen in on and take advantage of human affairs and of their common desire to abduct and detain human victims as slaves or companions. We are warned of their magical powers to manipulate the physical world and of their tendency to exploit human necessity by driving hard bargains – deals which they always insist upon fulfilling. Lastly and, of course, most usefully, we learn of the power that derives from knowing a faery's name. If you possess that secret, you will be able to overcome and escape the creature and its powers of enchantment.

On reflection, we realise that most traditional fairies are anonymous to us – the famous fairies in this book being a distinct exception to that rule. The rest closely guard their names from humans, precisely because they are a source of power. At the same time, however, the fairies are found to be often careless at protecting the key to their superiority, meaning that they are nearly always outwitted in the end. Welsh brownie Gwarwyn-a-throt exemplifies this: he is overheard by his intended victim foolishly repeating his name to himself, gloating that it is a secret – and so he is undone. In a similar example, also from Wales, possession of the fairy maiden's name constrained her to marry the human male who discovered it.[4]

Additionally, these stories all demonstrate how verse and rhyme are commonly used by faeries to formulate their secrets.[5] Luckily for their human victims, though, the verse form seems to compel the goblin-like characters to sing their secret to themselves, meaning that they are always overheard and undone. For example:

> "Little kens oor gude dame at hame,
> That Whuppity Stoorie is my name!"

> "Nimmy, nimmy not,
> My name's Tom Tit Tot" and,

> "Little did she know
> That Trwtyn Tratyn
> Is my name."

This last verse works much better in the original Welsh, reminding us too that rhythm and rhyme are essential to a good spell:

> "Bychan a wydda' hi
> Mai Trwtyn-Tratyn
> Yw f'enw i."

Because of the familiarity now of the German tale of Rumpelstiltskin, the ubiquity of which has displaced all the British originals, I give the text of several of the native versions, drawn from around the British Isles, and beginning with the

---

4 Rhys, *Celtic Folklore*, 45.
5 See my *Fairy Ballads & Rhymes*, 2020.

Suffolk dialect story of Tom Tit Trot. The sheer number of related tales indicates how significant the key themes once were to our perceptions of Faery – and how that information had to be passed on to subsequent generations.

THE STORY OF TOM TIT TOT

Once upon a time there was a woman, and she baked five pies. When they came out of the oven, they were that overbaked the crusts were too hard to eat, so she says to her daughter:

'Darter,' says she, 'put you them there pies on the shelf, and leave 'em there a little, and they'll come again.' She meant, you know, the crust would get soft.

But the girl, she says to herself: 'Well, if they'll come again, I'll eat 'em now.' And she set to work and ate 'em all, first and last.

Well, come supper-time the woman said: 'Go you, and get one o' them there pies. I dare say they've come again now.' The girl went and she looked, and there was nothing but the dishes. So back she came and says she: 'Noo, they ain't come again.'

'Not one of 'em?' says the mother.

'Not one of' 'em,' says she.

'Well, come again, or not come again,' said the woman, 'I'll have one for supper.'

'But you can't, if they ain't come,' said the girl.

'But I can,' says she. 'Go you, and bring the best of 'em.'

'Best or worst,' says the girl, 'I've ate 'em all, and you can't have one till that's come again.'

Well, the woman she was done, and she took her spinning to the door to spin, and as she span she sang:

'My darter ha' ate five, five pies today.

My darter ha' ate five, five pies today.'

The king was coming down the street, and he heard her sing, but what she sang he couldn't hear, so he stopped and said:

'What was that you were singing, my good woman?'

The woman was ashamed to let him hear what her daughter had been doing, so she sang, instead of that:

'My darter ha' spun five, five skeins today.

My darter ha' spun five, five skeins today.'

'Stars o' mine!' said the king, 'I never heard tell of anyone that could do that.' Then he said: 'Look you here, I want a wife, and I'll marry your daughter. But look you here,' says he, 'eleven months out of the year she shall have all she likes to eat, and all the gowns she likes to get, and all the company she likes to keep; but the last month of the year she'll have to spin five skeins every day, and if she don't I shall kill her.'

'All right,' says the woman; for she thought what a grand marriage that was. And as for the five skeins, when the time came, there'd be plenty of ways of getting out of it, and likeliest, he'd have forgotten all about it.

Well, so they were married. And for eleven months the girl had all she liked to eat, and all the gowns she liked to get, and all the company she liked to keep. But, when the time was getting over, she began to think about the skeins and to wonder if he had 'em in mind. But not one word did he say about 'em, and she thought he'd wholly forgotten 'em.

However, the last day of the last month he takes her to a room she'd never set eyes on before. There was nothing in it but a spinning-wheel and a stool. And says he: 'Now, my dear, here you'll be shut in tomorrow with some victuals and some flax, and if you haven't spun five skeins by the night, your head'll go off.' And away he went about his business.

Well, she was that frightened, she'd always been such a gatless girl, that she didn't so much as know how to spin, and what was she to do tomorrow with no one to come nigh her to help her? She sate down on a stool in the kitchen, and law! how she did cry! However, all of a sudden, she heard a sort of a knocking low down on the door. She upped and oped it, and what should she see but a small little black thing with a long tail. That looked up at her right curious, and that said:

'What are you a-crying for?'

'What's that to you?' says she.

'Never you mind,' that said, 'but tell me what you're a-crying for.'

'That won't do me no good if I do,' says she.

'You don't know that,' that said, and twirled that's tail round.

'Well,' says she, 'that won't do no harm, if that don't do no good,' and she upped and told about the pies, and the skeins, and everything.

'This is what I'll do,' says the little black thing. 'I'll come to your window every morning and take the flax and bring it spun at night.'

'What's your pay?' says she.

That looked out of the corner of that's eyes, and that said:

'I'll give you three guesses every night to guess my name, and if you haven't guessed it before the month's up you shall be mine.'

Well, she thought, she'd be sure to guess that's name before the month was up. 'All right,' says she, 'I agree.'

'All right,' that says, and law! how that twirled that's tail.

Well, the next day, her husband took her into the room, and there was the flax and the day's food.

'Now, there's the flax,' says he, 'and if that ain't spun up this night, off goes your head.' And then he went out and locked the door.

He'd hardly gone, when there was a knocking against the window. She upped and she opened it, and there sure enough was the little old thing sitting on the ledge.

'Where's the flax?' says he.

'Here it be,' says she. And she gave it to him.

Well, come the evening a knocking came again to the window. She upped and she opened it, and there was the little old thing with five skeins of flax on his arm.

'Here it be,' says he, and he gave it to her.

'Now, what's my name?' says he.

'What, is that Bill?' says she.

'Noo, that ain't,' says he, and he twirled his tail. 'Is that Ned?' says she.

'Noo, that ain't,' says he, and he twirled his tail. 'Well, is that Mark?' says she.

'Noo, that ain't,' says he, and he twirled his tail harder, and away he flew.

Well, when her husband came in, there were the five skeins ready for him. 'I see I shan't have to kill you tonight, my dear,' says he; 'you'll have your food and your flax in the morning,' says he, and away he goes.

Well, every day the flax and the food were brought, and every day that there little black impet used to come mornings and evenings. And all the day the girl sate trying to think of names to say to it when it came at night. But she never hit on the right one. And as it got towards the end of the month, the impet began to look so maliceful, and that twirled that's tail faster and faster each time she gave a guess.

At last it came to the last day but one. The impet came at night along with the five skeins, and that said:

'What, ain't you got my name yet?'

'Is that Nicodemus?' says she.

'Noo, 't ain't,' that says.

'Is that Sammle?' says she.

'Noo, 't ain't,' that says.

'A-well, is that Methusalem?' says she.

'Noo, 't ain't that neither,' that says.

Then that looks at her with that's eyes like a coal of fire, and that says: 'Woman, there's only tomorrow night, and then you'll be mine!' And away it flew. Well, she felt that horrid. However, she heard the king coming along the passage. In he came, and when he sees the five skeins, he says, says he:

'Well, my dear,' says he. 'I don't see but what you'll have your skeins ready tomorrow night as well, and as I reckon I shan't have to kill you, I'll have supper in here tonight.' So they brought supper, and another stool for him, and down the two sate.

Well, he hadn't eaten but a mouthful or so, when he stops and begins to laugh.

'What is it?' says she.

'A-why,' says he, 'I was out a-hunting today, and I got away to a place in the wood I'd never seen before. And there was an old chalk-pit. And I heard a kind of a sort of humming. So I got off my hobby, and I went right quiet to the pit, and I looked down. Well, what should there be but the funniest little black thing you ever set eyes on. And what was that doing, but that had a little spinning-wheel, and that was spinning wonderful fast, and twirling that's tail. And as that span that sang:

> 'Nimmy nimmy not
> My name's Tom Tit Tot.'

Well, when the girl heard this, she felt as if she could have jumped out of her skin for joy, but she didn't say a word.

Next day that there little thing looked so maliceful when he came for the flax. And when night came she heard that knocking against the window panes. She oped the window, and that come right in on the ledge. That was grinning from ear to ear, and Oo! that's tail was twirling round so fast.

'What's my name?' that says, as that gave her the skeins.

'Is that Solomon?' she says, pretending to be afeard.

'Noo, 'tain't,' that says, and that came further into the room.

'Well, is that Zebedee?' says she again.

'Noo, 'tain't,' says the impet. And then that laughed and twirled that's tail till you couldn't hardly see it.

'Take time, woman,' that says; 'next guess, and you're mine.' And that stretched out that's black hands at her.

Well, she backed a step or two, and she looked at it, and then she laughed out, and says she, pointing her finger at it:

> 'Nimmy nimmy not
> Your name's Tom Tit Tot.'

Well, when that heard her, that gave an awful shriek and away that flew into the dark, and she never saw it any more.

WELSH STORIES

Folklorist John Rhys recorded several fragmentary Welsh versions of the story of the fairy helper with the hidden name. He also endeavoured to make some sense of the names that these goblins tried to hide.

The story of Sili Go Dwt concerns a farmer's wife of Llaniestyn parish on the Lleyn peninsula in Gwynedd. This old woman was frequently visited by a fairy who used to borrow baking implements from her. The fairy was always given what she asked for and she always returned them with a loaf in thanks. However, one day she came to ask for the loan of the woman's wheel for spinning flax. When handing her this, the farmer's wife wished to know her visitor's name, given that she came so often, but the fairy refused to tell her. However, she was watched at her spinning, and was overheard singing to the whir of the wheel:

> *"Bychan a wydda' hi*
> *Mai Sìli go Dwt*
> *Yw f'enw I".*

> "Little did she know
> That Sili go Dwt
> Is my name."

The sprite here is a female fairy, rather than the male goblin of *Tom Tit Trot* and the Grimm's version. Spinning is again involved, although in this version no undertaking to do it for the farmer's wife is recorded and the spying on the fairy is simply a matter of curiosity rather than a question of life or death.[6]

Professor Rhys speculated that the fairy woman's name had been borrowed from English and that it meant the sprite who was 'somewhat tidy or natty' – the Welsh appropriating their word *twt* to make sense of English 'tot' as Tom Tit Tot. There are

---

6   See John Rhys, *Celtic Folklore*, vol.1, 229–30 & vol.2, 584–98.

other Welsh stories in which the fairy names derive from 'trot' or 'trut,' as with Trwtyn-Tratyn, which Rhys notes seems to be a male name, as is the Irish fairy Trit-a-Trot.[7]

To illustrate the more typical strand of tales, in which possession of the name is a vital, Rhys told a Monmouthshire story of a brownie-type being that was driven away from a farm by poor or disrespectful treatment at the hands of one of the maid servants. The brownie went to a nearby farm where he was much better treated, and where, in return, he undertook many different chores, including spinning yarn. The maid at the new farm wanted the spirit to appear to her or reveal his name, both of which he refused to do. One evening, though, she pretended to go out and then listened at the door as he was spinning:

> *Hi wardda'n iawn pe gwypa hi,*
> *Taw Gwarwyn-a-throt yw'm enw i.*

> How she would laugh, did she know
> That Gwarwyn-a-throt is my name!

As soon as she revealed that she knew his secret, the brownie abandoned his work and disappeared forever. Rhys again speculates about the meaning of the name, suggesting that it translates as 'white-necked with a trot.' The last element has no sense in Welsh and it could well be a borrowing of the English 'trot,' an elderly female.

It may also be worthwhile noting that, in the *Denham Tract* list of faeries, there is mention of 'tutgots.' Tut-gut, along with tut and tom-tit, were all words for a hobgoblin.[8] Around Spilsby in Lincolnshire, tut-got used to be a term denoting a person who had been abducted by goblins or fairies.[9] One example of a tut or tot is the Spittal Hill tut, a Lincolnshire form that took the form of a horse. Also described as a 'shagfoal,' it haunted the

---

7   See *Folklore*, vol.2, 1891, 132 & 246.

8   J.E. Brogden, *Provincial Words and Expressions Current in Lincolnshire*, 1866, 214.

9   Halliwell, *Dictionary of Archaic & Provincial Words*, vol.2, 1889.

road at the named location in Freiston parish, where it would mount travellers' horses and ride with them for a distance, all the time hugging them very tightly with its fore-legs. The tut was supposed to mark the site where, either, treasure was buried or a murder had been committed. On the Isle of Man there is record of a giant called Mollyndroat – perhaps Moll the Trot (or hobgoblin).[10]

There's also a variant of this type of Welsh story that features a sprite called Sili Ffrit. Once again, this name seems to be English in origin, being 'Silly Frit.' This simply means a silly sprite or apparition, using 'silly' in the same manner as the 'seelie court' of Scottish fairies. In this context, the word means 'lucky' or 'happy;' it is in part a euphemism to enable people to avoid saying 'fairy,' but it also acknowledges the different status of the faery folk.

WHUPPITY STOORIE

This is a Scottish take on the 'secret name' story, although the version reproduced here is taken from John Rhys, because he translated a lot of the more difficult or unfamiliar Scots dialect of Chambers' original.

"A farmer from Kittlerumpit disappeared, perhaps joining the army, and his wife was left alone with next to nothing to live on. She had very scant resources – and a baby boy at her breast. All her neighbours said they were sorry for her; but nobody helped her – which is a sadly common situation. Howsoever, the goodwife had a sow, and that was her only consolation; for the sow was soon to farrow, and she hoped for a good litter.

However, we all know hope is fallacious. One day the woman went to the sty to fill the sow's trough and there she found the sow lying on her back, grunting and groaning, and ready to give up the ghost.

---

10 P. Thompson, *History & Antiquities of Boston*, 1856, 736; Mona Douglas, 'Gods, Sprites & Fairies,' in *Journal of the Folk Song Society*, vol.7, 1924; see too my *Beyond Faery*, 2020.

This was a fresh and serious blow to the poor woman and she sat down on the knocking-stone, with her bairn on her knee, and cried sorer than ever she did for the loss of her own goodman [husband].[11]

Now, the cottage of Kittlerumpit was built on a brae, with a large fir-wood behind it, of which you may hear more ere we go far on. So the goodwife, when she was wiping her eyes, chanced to look down the brae; and what did she see but an old woman, almost like a lady, coming slowly up the road. She was dressed in green, all except for a short white apron and a black velvet hood, and a steeple-crowned beaver hat on her head. She had a long walking-staff, as long as herself, in her hand – the sort of staff that old men and old women helped themselves with long ago, but which no-one carried any longer.

When the goodwife saw the green gentlewoman near her, she rose and made a curtsy; and "Madam," quoth she, weeping, "I am one of the most misfortunate women alive."

"I don't wish to hear pipers' news and fiddlers' tales, goodwife," quoth the green woman. "I know you have lost your goodman – we had worse losses at the [battle of] Sheriff Muir [during the Jacobite rebellion in 1715] and I know that your sow is unco sick. Now what will you give me if I cure her?"

"Anything your ladyship's madam likes," quoth the witless goodwife, never guessing whom she had to deal with.

"Let us wet thumbs on that bargain," quoth the green woman – so thumbs were wetted, I warrant you; and into the sty madam marches. She looked at the sow with a long stare, and then began to mutter to herself what the goodwife couldn't well understand; but she said it sounded like –

Pitter patter,
Holy Water.[12]

---

11 The knocking stone is a concave boulder used for getting the husk of grain.
12 In Northern English and Scots dialects, 'water' is pronounced 'watter' so that we have a proper rhyme in this charm.

Then the woman in green took out of her pocket a wee bottle, with something like oil in it, and she rubbed the sow with it above the snout, behind the ears, and on the tip of the tail. "Get up, beast," quoth the green woman. This was no sooner said than done: up jumped the sow with a grunt, and away to her trough for her breakfast.

The goodwife of Kittlerumpit was a joyful goodwife now, and would have kissed the very hem of the green woman's gown-tail; but she wouldn't let her. "I am not so fond of ceremonies," quoth she; "but now that I have righted your sick beast, let us end our settled bargain. You will not find me an unreasonable, greedy body – I like ever to do a good turn for a small reward: all I ask, and will have, is that baby boy at your bosom."

The goodwife of Kittlerumpit, who now knew her customer, gave a shrill cry like a stuck swine. The green woman was a fairy, no doubt; so she prayed, and cried, and begged, and scolded; but none of it did any good. "You may spare your din," quoth the fairy, "screaming as if I was as deaf as a door-nail; but this I'll let you know – I cannot, by the law we live under, take your bairn till the third day; and not then, if you can tell me my right name." So, madam goes away round the pig-sty end, and the goodwife falls down in a swoon behind the knocking-stone.[13]

Ah well, the goodwife of Kittlerumpit could not sleep any that night for crying, and all the next day the same, cuddling her bairn till she nearly squeezed its breath out; but on the second day she decided to take a walk in the wood I told you of; so with the bairn in her arms, she set out, and went far in amongst the trees, where there was an old quarry-hole, grown over with grass, and with a bonny spring well in the middle of it. Before she came very near, she heard the whirring of a flax wheel, and a voice singing a song; so the woman crept quietly among the bushes, and peeped over the brow of the quarry; and what did she see but the green fairy tearing away at her wheel, and singing like any precentor:

---

13 Whether fairy law mandates such a delay, or whether it is just a dramatic pause used by storytellers to create tension, is unknown.

> Little kens our guid dame at hame,
> That Whuppity Stoorie is my name.

"Ha, ha!" thought the woman, "I've got the mason's word at last; the devil give them joy that told it!" So, she went home far lighter than she came out, as you may well guess, and laughing like a madcap with the thought of cheating the old green fairy.

Ah well, you must know that this goodwife was a jocose woman, and ever merry when her heart was not very sorely overladen. So she thought to have some sport with the fairy; and at the appointed time she put the bairn behind the knocking-stone, and sat on the stone herself. Then she pulled her cap over her left ear and twisted her mouth on the other side, as if she were weeping; and an ugly face she made, you may be sure. She hadn't long to wait, for up the brae climbed the green fairy, neither lame nor lazy, and long ere she got near the knocking-stone she screamed out – "Goodwife of Kittlerumpit, you know well what I come for – stand and deliver!"

The woman pretended to cry even harder than before, and wrung her hands, and fell on her knees, with "Och, sweet madam mistress, spare my only bairn, and take the wretched sow!"

"The devil take the sow, for my part," quoth the fairy; "I come not here for swine's flesh. Don't be contramawcious, huzzy, but give me the child instantly!"

"Ochone, dear lady mine," quoth the crying goodwife; "forgo my poor bairn, and take me myself!"[14]

"The devil is in the daft jade," quoth the fairy, looking like the far end of a fiddle; "I'll bet she is clean demented. Who in all the earthly world, with half an eye in his head, would ever meddle with the likes of thee?"

I reckon this set up the woman of Kittlerumpit's bristle: for though she had two blear eyes and a long red nose besides, she thought herself as bonny as the best of them. So she sprung off her knees, set the top of her cap straight, and with her two

---

14 'Ochone' is an expression equivalent to 'woe is me.'

hands folded before her, she made a curtsy down to the ground, and, "In troth, fair madam," quoth she, "I might have had the wit to know that the likes of me is not fit to tie the worst shoe-strings of the high and mighty princess, Whuppity Stoorie."

If a flash of gunpowder had come out of the ground it couldn't have made the fairy leap higher than she did; then down she came again plump on her shoe-heels; and whirling round, she ran down the brae, screeching for rage, like an owl chased by the witches.

The goodwife of Kittlerumpit laughed till she was like to split; then she took up her bairn and went into her house, singing to it all the way:

> "A goo and a gitty, my bonny wee tyke,
> Ye'se noo ha'e your four-oories;
> Sin' we've gien Nick a bane to pyke,
> Wi' his wheels and his Whuppity Stoories."[15]

In conclusion to the story of Whuppity Story, we may note that Robert Chambers suggested that the fairy's name came from the word 'whip' combined with the Scots word for dust whirlwind, a known method of fairy travel.

Finally, John Rhys appended to this another Scottish story, from Mochdrum in Wigtownshire. "A wife was in great distress, because her husband kept giving her large amounts of flax to spin with very short deadlines, so that the work was beyond human power. A fairy came to her rescue, taking the flax away and promising to bring it back spun by the date set, provided the woman could tell the fairy's name. The woman's distress was then as great as before, but the fairy was overheard saying as she spun, 'Little does the guidwife wot, my name is Marget Tot.' So, the woman got her flax returned spun by the day; and the fairy went up the chimney in a blaze of fire as the result of rage and disappointment."[16]

---

15 The 'oories' seem to be fears or worries; 'Nick' is the devil.
16 Cited from the British Association's *Papers of the Liverpool Meeting*, 1896, 613.

In summary, a key figure in fairyland has always been the dangerous individual who offers help – at too high a price. We are warned repeatedly of the perils of entering into bargains with fairies, even where this may be justified by the considerable craft skills they offer and the sanction that the human otherwise faces. Fortunately, though, with luck and wisdom the unfortunate humans can discover the knowledge that redresses the balance and saves their skin.

CHAPTER TWELVE

Nimue and Merlin

The Arthurian myths are full of powerful females, some mortal, some of fairy origin. Guinevere and Morgan le Fay are humans, although Morgan has studied magic deeply and is 'fay' in the sense of being an enchantress. In contrast, the Lady of the Lake, protector of Sir Launcelot and provider of Excalibur, and the beauteous Nimue are both supernatural beings. Indeed, in many respects the Lady of the Lake seems identical with Nimue/ Niniane/ Viviane. Both are fairy women with magical powers who operate mysteriously on the fringes of the stories of Arthur's court.[1] However, the latter character has evolved to become the better known of the pair. This was because she came to be more distinctly modelled by writers and because she was accused, in particular, of treacherously seducing and imprisoning Arthur's wizard Merlin, an act which helped precipitate the end of the entire golden age of Arthur's reign.

OLDER ACCOUNTS

The story of Merlin and Nimue can be briefly outlined. Successive authors have embroidered these basics, but the core is simple and short.

Malory described how Merlin "fel in a dotage on the damosel" Nimue, who flattered and charmed him, not because she felt any affection for the old wizard, but because she desired his arcane knowledge. He, though, "was so sore assotted upon her that he might not be from her." When this "damosel of the lake" left the court, Merlin followed her.[2]

---

1 Whom Lewis Spence connects with the Welsh moon goddess Rhiannon (*British fairy origins*, p.147).
2 *Morte d'Arthur* c.58.

In *Polyolbion* Michael Drayton described what followed almost inevitably from the elderly magician's sad obsession. He described how Merlin,

> "by loving of an elf,
> For all his wondrous skills was cozened of himself:
> For, walking with his Fay, her to the rock he brought
> In which he oft his nigromancies wrought.
> And going in thereat, his magics to have shown,
> She stopt the cavern's mouth with an enchanted stone,
> Whose cunning strongly crossed, amazed while he did stand,
> She captive him conveyed unto Fairyland."[3]

These are the essential elements of Nimue's career and they portray her wholly negatively. Even so, there is one incident which sheds a more favourable light upon her. According to some accounts, when Arthur has been gravely wounded in the battle of Camlann, he is taken to the shore of a lake or sea. Firstly, his sword, Excalibur, is returned to the Lady of the Lake by being cast into the waters. Then a ship appears, bearing Morgan le Fay and other women, amongst whom are the Queen of 'Northgalis' (North Wales), the Queen of the Wasteland, and Nimue. They carry Arthur away to the Isle of Avalon where Morgan cultivates those healing herbs with which she will treat his mortal injuries.

In fact, in the Middle English poem *Sir Gawain and the Green Knight* Morgan and Nimue are confounded together and her character as either fairy woman or goddess seems as uncertain as her identity:

> "Through the might of Morgan le Fay, who remains in my
>   house,
> Through the wiles of her witchcraft, a lore well-learned –
> Many of the magical arts of Merlin she acquired
> For she lavished fervent love long ago
> On that susceptible sage; certainly, your knights know

---

3 Drayton, Song IV.

Of their fame.
So 'Morgan the Goddess'
She accordingly became;
The proudest she can oppress
And to her purpose tame."[4]

VICTORIAN REVIVAL

After Malory, there were nearly four centuries of neglect of the legend until Matthew Arnold revived it in 1852 by way of an account told by a character in the course of another story. Vivien was, to Merlin, "that false fay, his friend."

> "She looked so fair, that learned wight
> Forgot his craft and his best wits took flight
> And he grew fond and eager to obey
> His mistress, use her empire as she may."[5]

Vivien was fully restored to public consciousness by Alfred, Lord Tennyson. The poem *Merlin and Vivien* lies at the heart of his Arthurian epic, *The Idylls of the King*, which he published as an entire work in 1872, although *Vivien* had been composed in about 1859.

In Tennyson's epic, Vivien is cast alongside Mordred as one of the committed enemies of Arthur's court. She conspires over an extended period to disrupt his reign and to topple him from his throne and, as a traitor to the realm, she is variously described as a liar, wily, plotting and lurking. Her subterfuge and cunning are facilitated by the fact that men are blinded to her true character: she is at the same time beautiful and sexy:

> "A twist of gold round her hair; a robe
> Of samite without price, that more exprest
> Than hid her, clung about her lissome limbs…"

---

4 Lines 2446–2455.
5 Arnold, *Merlin and the Fay Vivian* in 'Tristram and Iseult,' in *Empedocles on Etna and Other Poems*, 1852.

Men are distracted by her skin-tight dresses, most fatally Merlin, who despite his great age and the enormous disparity in their years, falls helplessly in love with her. This was, of course, Vivien's plan, because she wishes to learn from him a secret charm "Of woven paces and of waving hands." This is a powerful and dangerous enchantment and Merlin, even in his obsessed condition, still hesitates to disclose it to her.

However, the pair leave the court together and travel to the Forest of Broceliande in Brittany, where Vivien wears him down with promises of love and devotion. Eventually she triumphs:

> "For Merlin, overtalk'd and overworn,
> Had yielded, told her all the charm, and slept.
> Then, in one moment, she put forth the charm
> Of woven paces and of waving hands,
> And in the hollow oak as he lay as dead,
> And lost to life and use and name and fame."

Vivien dismisses the imprisoned old man as a fool – and abandons him there.

Coincidentally, the same year that Tennyson first wrote his poem on the subject, Scot Robert Buchanan composed *Merlin's Tomb*. It is a very similar tale of doomed love. Viviane lures the old magus into a wood and they sit beneath a fairy tree:

> "The spot was fair, the lovers fain;
> Beneath that hawthorn tree
> Sir Merlin and fair Viviane
> Disport them lovingly."

Things are not what they seem, however. He falls asleep and she seizes the opportunity to use the spell she has just coaxed from him:

> "The lady looked – 'He slumbers well,'
> (She thought – ah, woe the hour!)

'Now is the time to prove my spell –
My spell of wondrous power!"

Gently Sir Merlin's head she's placed,
And slowly, on the ground;
Then muttering, with her wimple traced
A ring the hawthorn round.

Nine times that magic ring she made –
Nine times that spell she spoke,
Then on her lap the slumberer laid;
But when Sir Merlin woke,

He looked a wild, he looked a long
Upon his prison-bower;
It seemed a castle fair and strong,
Begirt with trench and tower.

Sir Merlin frown'd, Sir Merlin sigh'd,
Fair Viviane laughed the while;
'Such fortune still must fool betide
Will trust a woman's wile!'"

Just like Tennyson, Buchanan conceives of the powerful spell as a charm involving both words and movement. He adds further to the fairy aura of his poem by adding a hawthorn tree as the venue for the wizard's downfall.

Since the appearance of Tennyson's great work, Vivien has fascinated many other writers with her fatal, feminine power over men. French poet Jean Lorraine composed an entire verse drama about *Viviane* in 1885, which concludes with Merlin being entombed asleep in 'shadows' using dance and gestures. The fairy woman does this to satisfy her long-nurtured rancour against him, we are told.[6]

---

6 Similar 'evil Viviens' are found in W.B. Yeats, *Time and the Witch Vivien*, 1889; Ernest Rhys, *The Death of Merlin*, 1898 and Ethel Watts Mumford, *Merlin and Vivien – a Lyrical Drama*, 1907.

Two more recent writers treated this fairy temptress rather more benignly. In Edward Arlington Robinson's verse epic, *Merlin* (1917), Vivian is the daughter of a fairy and she "holds him with her love, they say." Wilfrid Scawen Blunt's *To Nimue* (1914) is written as an internal monologue by Merlin, who had loved Nimue as a child but thought himself recovered from his passion. He meets her again as a grown woman, and quickly weakens in the face of her adult charms when he finds that she now returns his love.

The story of Merlin and Nimue also had great appeal to painters; understandably, given that it enabled them to juxtapose young, feminine beauty with hoary age. Sir Edward Burne-Jones, for example, twice tackled the story. In both versions, his Nimue has possession of Merlin's book of spells; in *The Beguiling of Merlin* (1870–74), he places the pair beneath the blossoming hawthorn tree, just as Buchanan described. In addition, the sexual obsession felt by the older man for the girl is captured very well in the recumbent Merlin's longing look. Other depictions include those by Arthur Rackham (from *The Romance of King Arthur*, 1917) and by Frank Cadogan Cowper. His *Damsel of the Lake: Nimue the Enchantress*, painted in 1924, emphasises the pride and beauty of the fairy. She sits alone, admiring her hair in a mirror in an almost mermaid-like fashion. She is dressed in a robe of flowing white satin, which is embroidered with a spiral pattern on the chest that draws attention to her breasts. A deer, with a golden crown about its neck, sits at her feet. Isolated in a twilight landscape, Nimue is at once alluring yet menacing. Eleanor Fortescue Brickdale's 1911 *Vivien* is vampish in a tiger skin mantle whilst H. J. Ford chose a leopard's pelt for her; American illustrator Howard Pyle's *Enchantress Vivien* has a low-cut dress and an enigmatic gypsy look, weighed down with jewellery; John Smith Moyr in 1875 and Louis Rhead in 1898 made her into something of an exotic dancer. In all these depictions, her magical and sexual power are to the fore.

There have been many poetic, and even more prose versions, of this story since Victorian times, all of them reworking the same basic themes, but as last indications of the pervasive influence of the image of the spiteful and lovely fay maiden, and of the inspiration provided to other artists and writers by the individual works I have discussed, I quote firstly *The Thorn Tree* (1911), a poem by American author Madison Julius Cawein. He tells us –

"Of the Lady of the Fountain, whom the faery people know,
With her limbs of samite whiteness and her hair of golden
   glow...
She whose Vivien charms were mistress of the magic Merlin
   knew,
That could change the dew to glow-worms and the glow-
   worms into dew.
There's a thorn tree in the forest, and the faeries know the
   tree,
With its branches gnarled and wrinkled as a face with
   sorcery;
But the Maytime brings it clusters of a rainy fragrant white,
Like the bloom-bright brows of beauty or a hand of lifted
   light.
And all day the silence whispers to the sun-ray of the morn
How the bloom is lovely Vivien and how Merlin is the
   thorn:
How she won the doting wizard with her naked loveliness
Till he told her daemon secrets that must make his magic
   less.
How she charmed him and enchanted in the thorn-tree's
   thorns to lie
Forever with his passion that should never dim or die...
How she stooped to kiss the pathos of an elf-lock of his
   beard,
In a mockery of parting and mock pity of his weird:
But her magic had forgotten that who bends to give a kiss

Will but bring the curse upon them of the person whose it
   is:
So the silence tells the secret. And at night the faeries see
How the tossing bloom is Vivien, who is struggling to be
   free,
In the thorny arms of Merlin, who forever is the tree."

We might leave Nimue and Merlin united in their fate, then, both betrayed by their own magic, but the pathos and tragedy of their story continues to attract authors, even today. Modern-day internet poet John Bliven Morin was drawn again to the blind passion of older lover for a young woman. In the *Love Song of Ambrosius* (which uses an ancient Welsh name for the magician) the wizard willingly invites her into his domain, oblivious to the threat she poses and seeking to assuage any fears she may feel with promises to share his secret knowledge and his spell books:

"And in exchange you offer love,
Which I have never known;
Your tender kiss, your gentle touch,
And that soft moan.

And should you take my power
And leave me powerless
Still I give it willingly
For your caress."

Nimue/ Vivien embodies both the otherness and the fatal sexual allure of the fairy lover; this combination remains as irresistible as ever. We see this even in the modern character of Tinker Bell, the last famous fairy to be discussed.

CHAPTER THIRTEEN

Tinker Bell

The final famous fairy we must mention is the least traditional of all. This is J.M. Barrie's Tinker Bell, a late arrival on the scene who has quickly established herself as almost the archetypal female fairy.

Tinker Bell is a literary creation, who appeared first in Barrie's 1904 play *Peter Pan* and subsequently in his 1911 novelisation of the story, *Peter and Wendy*. She is the author's invention, but she nevertheless incorporates some traditional fairy elements into her character and conduct. Barrie also mentioned fairies in his wider 'Peter Pan' corpus, in books such as *The Little White Bird* (1902) and *Peter Pan in Kensington Gardens* (1906).

TINK & TRADITION

First and foremost, Tinker Bell is diminutive, as tradition had come to expect. In fact, all of the fairies in Barrie's stories are small, but Tinker Bell is described most evocatively as being "no longer than your hand, but still growing."[1] Furthermore, like many native British faes, she has her own language. Barrie has her speaking a tongue that is incomprehensible to human children (although Peter Pan has learned it). Her speech is said to be like "the loveliest tinkle of golden bells," but it's also described as high-pitched squeaking. This description fits well with many older eye witness accounts of fairy speech.[2] We are told, furthermore, that babies are born able to speak the fairy language but quickly forget it as they grow and learn their parents' tongue.[3]

---

1 *Peter & Wendy* c.3.
2 See my *British Fairies* c.3.
3 *Peter & Wendy* cc.3 & 10; *Kensington Gardens* cc.4 & 5; *Little White Bird* cc.XVI & XXI.

Lastly, and most memorably, there is Tinker Bell's bad temperament. This is seen in *Peter Pan* in the fairy's vindictive jealously towards Wendy and in the use generally by Barrie's fairies of physical chastisements. In this respect, too, Barrie's fairies are very authentic to British tradition.[4] They tweak Peter's nose when he sleeps across a fairy path; they 'mischief' those they take against. In the novel *Peter Pan in Kensington Gardens*, Barrie explains that "Nearly all the nasty accidents you meet with in the Gardens occur because the fairies have taken an ill-will against you and so it behoves you to be careful what you say about them ..." "If the fairies see you ... they will mischief you – stab you to death, or compel you to nurse their children, or turn you into something tedious, like an evergreen oak."[5]

Of Tinker Bell's character specifically, Barrie explained that she "was not all bad: or, rather, she was all bad just now, but, on the other hand, sometimes she was all good. Fairies have to be one thing or the other, because being so small they unfortunately have room for one feeling only at a time. They are, however, allowed to change, only it must be a compete change."[6] For readers familiar with traditional fairy lore, these accounts of abductions, violence and the need to speak circumspectly in their presence will once again sound very familiar.

TEMPTRESS TINK

Tink herself is introduced thus: she was "exquisitely gowned in a skeleton leaf cut low and square, through which her figure could be seen to the best advantage. She was slightly inclined to *embonpoint*."[7] Later Wendy describes her cattily as "an abandoned little creature" and that aura of wickedness

---

4 *British Fairies* c.20.
5 *Kensington Gardens* c.5.
6 *Peter & Wendy* c.4.
7 *Peter & Wendy* c.3.

or wantonness pervades the character.[8] All in all, Tinker Bell appears to be an adult – or nearly so: recall that Barrie tells us that she is "still growing," perhaps a subtle suggestion of an ongoing sexual maturation – those curves are getting curvier. Worse still, she is "quite a common fairy" and is not very polite, using "offensive" and "impudent" language to Wendy in their squabble over Peter.[9] This might be read as sexual possessiveness, or it might be the childhood exclusiveness of 'the best friend.' Given that Tinker Bell is prepared to try to kill her love rival, the former seems most likely.

Tink's sexual allure and her strong attachment to her chosen male are strongly reminiscent of the dangerous fairy lovers of folklore, creatures such as the Scottish *leanan sith*, of whom Barrie might have been aware. The motif of sexual jealousy between Tinkerbell and Wendy (who is just feeling the first stirrings of maternal protectiveness) is one of the most interesting elements of the *Peter Pan* stories. It might be thought to accord ill with Barrie's claims for a natural bond between fairies and very young children, but perhaps in that very contradiction we find a true expression of the contrariness of Faery.

All these familiar folklore elements notwithstanding, significant aspects of the character and abilities of Tinker Bell and the other fairies in Barrie's stories have nothing at all to do with British tradition. Probably Barrie's most notable invention is fairy-dust, which enables the fairies to fly. It covers Tinker Bell and rubs off; we are not told exactly what it is, but there are possible links to the sandman, as well, perhaps, to the properties of fern seed found in folk magical tradition.[10]

When *Peter Pan* originally performed in the theatre, Tinker Bell's sexuality and feminine corporeality was *not* an issue; instead, she lost any physical form at all. The problem of depicting her in the play was solved by means of a flickering,

---

8   *Peter & Wendy* c.10.
9   *Peter & Wendy* cc.3 & 10.
10 *Peter & Wendy* c.3.

dancing light, which was reflected onto the stage using a mirror. This conceit has been very influential since (along too, perhaps, with some confusion over the nature of 'fairy lights' on Christmas trees, in which I take the 'fairy' element merely to denote tiny size, as against any supernatural aspect). The conception of fairies as moving points of light seems much more common now than it was in the recorded folklore preceding *Peter Pan* (although it was not entirely absent) and this development could well be ascribed to the influence of Barrie's stage play. Be that as it may, Tinker Bell's future place in popular consciousness was definitively secured by another sort of flickering light.

In the Walt Disney Studios cartoon of *Peter Pan* (1953), Tinker Bell was animated, but had no dialogue. The character has since become one of the company's most important branding icons, in part because she symbolises 'the magic of Disney.' She has featured in television and film commercials and in the opening credits to television programmes, sprinkling dust with a wand in reference to the 'magic' of Disney's films (although the 1953 animated version of Tinker Bell never actually used a wand). So popular has Tink proved that a number of spin-off films have been made featuring her as sole star. Her iconic status is confirmed by the fact that several witnesses reporting encounters to the recent *Fairy Census* explicitly compare what they saw to Tinkerbell or to Disney.[11]

Barrie was clear about the womanly reality of his Tinker Bell. The cartoon version was faithful to this, although she lost the plumpness and, in fact, seems rather concerned by the size of her hips.[12] It is often said that the original model for the cartoon character was Marilyn Monroe; in truth, animator Marc Davis derived his inspiration from another actress, Margaret Kerry. Davis drew Tinker Bell as young, white and attractive, with a pronounced hour-glass figure, her blonde hair in a bun, her eyes oversized and blue and her lips scarlet. She is clad in an extremely short green dress and green slippers and

11 See for instance Young, *Census*, numbers 61, 100 & 122.
12 In the scene with the mirror.

trails fairy dust when she flies (with her gauzy wings). In this overtly sexualised form, Tinker Bell is probably one of the most authentic surviving aspects of Barrie's work. Undoubtedly, Tink helped to cement the image of the pretty, tiny, winged female fairy in the public imagination. She has become a firm children's favourite, and the Disney vision of her is an icon in its own right. As I stated at the start of this chapter, Tink is now (for many) the exemplar of how fairies look. It's intriguing, nonetheless, how much she preserves of the original folklore fairy in her character *and* looks.

Conclusion

As I suggested in the Foreword, British faerylore is a mix of tradition and innovation. The consequence of this process of accretion and absorption over centuries is that many of the best known faes are actually neither traditional nor native. They have been recruited into the ranks of Faery from outside – or they have been invented by novelists and playwrights: so successfully in fact that we accept that as part of our national heritage when they are, from a purist perspective, impostors.

As is the case with British history, successive waves of invaders have tended to overwhelm and subsume previous inhabitants. In just the same way, Oberon, Titania and Tinker Bell have overwhelmed those who held sway before them. Mab and Arthur have not been entirely forgotten, but they now survive in the shadow of those that followed them. Perhaps today something comparable is starting to take place and, in a century or more, people might regard Arwen and Legolas as typical examples of the archetypal British elf. We shall see; mythology can be a story we tell ourselves and to which we all contribute.